M000158425

Night's Promise

Sandy Lynn

A Samhain Publishing, Ltd. publication.

Samhain Publishing, Ltd.
2932 Ross Clark Circle, #384
Dothan, AL 36301
www.samhainpublishing.com

Night's Promise
Copyright © 2006 by Sandy Lynn
Print ISBN: 1-59998-289-7
Digital ISBN: 1-59998-082-7

Editing by Angie James
Cover by Scott Carpenter

This book is a work of fiction. The names, characters, places, and incidents are products of the writer's imagination or have been used fictitiously and are not to be construed as real. Any resemblance to persons, living or dead, actual events, locale or organizations is entirely coincidental.

All Rights Are Reserved. No part of this book may be used or reproduced in any manner whatsoever without written permission, except in the case of brief quotations embodied in critical articles and reviews.

First Samhain Publishing, Ltd. electronic publication: August 2006
First Samhain Publishing, Ltd. print publication: November 2006

Dedication

I would like to dedicate this book to my friends. Jess, without you, I don't think Duncan would have come to life like he did. Ferra, thank you for giving me a kick in the butt when it was needed. And to the wonderful Joyous, I thank you for being honest with me and giving me your opinions.

I'd also like to thank my wonderful editor for helping me make this book all that it could be.

Prologue

Melissa smiled as she watched Gareth follow La and Bram to the back room. Over half the club heard La say she loved him.

He deserves it, she thought, enjoying the fact that her brother would be happy. For almost a week her brother and La had bounced back and forth between being lovers and fighting. They couldn't seem to decide between the two states. No matter which "mode" they were in, though, it was clear they still wanted each other.

No other woman had ever captured her brother's attention or heart like Lalita did. She would be his heaven and his hell, but it was obvious she felt the same fire for him. Melissa was no sorceress, but she could practically see the sparks—the flames—jump between them whenever they touched.

Turning toward the table, her smile dimmed as she saw the bleached blonde still sitting there.

The least she could do for her brother would be to make sure Diane knew she didn't stand a chance with Gareth. She didn't want anyone to get hurt, but more importantly she didn't want her brother's good mood ruined by this wench's attempt to cling to him.

Melissa headed for the table, her smile becoming forced as she sat down, her hands smoothing her jeans. "You know those two are together, don't you?" she asked, deciding to go for the direct approach.

"Perhaps. But that doesn't mean I have to stop speaking to him."

"Do you *want* to get beaten up?" Diane's head jerked, turning toward her as though she had just been threatened. *Which, I sort of just did…* Staring at the other woman, Melissa shook her head. "Lalita doesn't play those games. And neither does Gareth. They're together now, so you really should leave him alone."

"Well, my business with him isn't done yet."

"Your business? What business?" she asked icily.

"You're his sister. Maybe you can tell me what he's like and then I can leave him alone all the quicker." Diane seemed to be talking to herself when she added, "I don't think Mr. Long would actually care if we weren't dating…"

Melissa's full attention was focused on the blonde as soon as she heard that name. *It's a coincidence. There could be a hundred people in this city with that name,* she tried to convince herself. Trying to fight off the cold shiver and biting back a retort of where the woman could go when she left, Melissa forced herself to respond politely. "What do you want to know?"

During her silence, Diane seemed to have reconsidered. "Never mind. I don't think my…friend would appreciate me having any help. I guess you're just stuck with me for a while longer."

Trying to ignore the icy fingers that continued to crawl up her spine, Melissa asked, "Can I at least know his name?"

Diane sat there, her back straighter and a smug smile on her face. She knew she had the upper hand now that Melissa was curious.

Catching Mona's eye, Melissa waved her over. A wave of relief swept through her when her friend nodded and approached the table.

"I believe you were just going to tell me what your friend's name was," Melissa said to Diane, her voice commanding as Mona sat on the other side of the blonde.

"No, I wasn't. Trust me, you don't want to make an enemy of me. Or my friend." Diane's voice was self-important, a challenge in her eyes taunting Melissa to make her tell her secret.

Melissa turned her attention on Mona, using her eyes to plead for help.

"I assume there is a good reason you're asking me to do this?" Mona tilted her head to the side slightly, her eyes never leaving Melissa's.

"Gods, I hope not." Even she could hear the desperation in her voice.

Diane looked between the women and opened her mouth to say something, but Mona had made her decision. Placing her hand on Diane's arm, she closed her eyes. When they opened again, Mona's pupils were much larger than normal and Diane had a slightly dazed look on her face. Mona gave an obviously fake laugh and began to speak as though they had been deep in conversation.

"Oh, Goddess, I don't think I've ever heard anything funnier. By the Lady, if I laugh any harder, I'm afraid I'm going to embarrass myself."

Diane looked confused, but an easy smile tilted on her lips. She seemed not to notice the hand still grasping her arm. "I'm telling you, I couldn't believe he said that to me."

"What about the other guy...what was his name...the one you mentioned earlier?" Melissa added, joining the contrived conversation.

"Which one?" Diane asked Mona, taking a sip from her glass with her free hand.

"The one that told you about Gareth."

"Oh, you mean Travis? You don't want to know about him, he's no fun and somewhat creepy, to be honest."

"Travis?" Mona asked.

"Yeah, Travis Long. But trust me, you do not want to look him up unless you have to. He might actually be handsome if he hadn't let himself go so badly..."

At the mention of that name, the blood drained from Melissa's face. She'd always suspected he'd try to find her, no matter how many times Gareth swore she would never have to see him again.

"Why did...Travis," her voice caught on the name, "send you to find Gareth?"

"I'm not sure. He just asked me to gather some info on him. To tell the truth, he gave off the vibe that your brother was some kind of monster. I so was not expecting such a hottie."

"What were you supposed to find out?" Melissa steered the conversation back to what she wanted—no, what she needed to know.

"He told me to find out any weaknesses." Diane shrugged. "He says he has some unfinished business with him. He told me to do whatever it takes to get information on Gareth. That he was a criminal, that he stole something very valuable. Whatever your brother did to him, he got Travis seriously pissed."

Shaking her head to clear away the unwanted thoughts, pushing horrible memories back to where they could do her no harm, Melissa forced herself to look at Diane again. Mona had released her and Diane seemed to have no memory of the conversation they'd just been having. Mona was watching Melissa carefully, but she could not contain her emotions.

Rage flooding her body, she snarled, "Stay away from my brother, you bitch."

"And just who's going to make me? You?" Diane laughed.

Years of pent up frustration erupted and before she even knew what she was doing, Melissa's hands grabbed both sides of Diane's head. With her fingers gripping hair, she slammed the other woman down on the hard surface of the table over and over again.

"Whoa." A man's voice came from behind her.

Strong hands forced her to release her grip on Diane's head before quickly dragging her backward, away from her prey. For a moment Melissa wondered if Gareth had come back, if he was the one pulling her away from this woman who threatened to tear her family apart.

"Calm down, beautiful, just calm down," the man crooned in her ear.

"Duncan, I don't know what happened." Mona stared at Melissa as though she'd never seen her before.

Melissa struggled against the arms, intent on hurting the monster who was so determined on destroying any shred of happiness she could have. The monster she'd thought she left in the past where he could no longer hurt her.

But when she looked at the once smug bitch sitting beside her friend, she didn't see a bleached blonde holding her head with delicate hands and perfectly manicured nails. Instead, she saw a tall man, his face rough from three days without shaving, limp, dull, dirty blond hair hanging into his face and a sneer that promised she would pay dearly for denying him what he wanted.

Shaking her head, Melissa's vision cleared and she saw the annoying blonde woman once again.

Chapter One

"Mom, I don't want to be a cheerleader. All the other girls in my class are trying out. I prefer to march to my own beat."

"I know sweetie, but a girl your age shouldn't be here trying to care for her mother. You should be out having fun, walking through the mall. I just want you to be happy."

Melissa looked at her mother's pale skin. She seemed to grow weaker every day, despite Melissa's best efforts to nurse her mother back to health. "I am happy. I love spending time with you. I know, why don't we read? I got *Dracula* from the school library."

Her mother gave a weak laugh. "You and your fascination with vampires. I would love to listen to you read for a little while." She patted the bed beside her.

Melissa obeyed, sitting close to her mother. Of course she was fascinated. They were never sick, never caught diseases…vampires didn't waste away in front of their daughter. With a smile, she snuggled closer to her mother and began to read the story.

Time flew as she read, until she was jerked from her story by the door slamming shut. Her mother had fallen asleep more than a chapter ago, but she had continued to read aloud, the process soothing Melissa as much as it had seemed to help ease her mother's pain.

Her stepfather stormed into the house, he always did, and she had only just put the book away when he slinked into the room.

"How's she doing?" Travis asked, giving her mother the barest glance.

"She's doing better, I think. She seemed to be in less pain."

"Don't fool yourself, girl. She's not going to get better. I don't understand why you waste your time on foolish dreams. Now, what's for supper?"

Melissa wanted to scream at him. To tell him that wishing for her mother to get better wasn't a foolish dream. She wanted to hit him and tell him he could fix his own supper.

Instead, she placed a gentle kiss on her mother's cheek and stood. She knew that if she said anything, the only outcome would be an argument, their raised voices forcing her mother from her peaceful sleep. Unable to bear the thought of disturbing her, Melissa simply bowed her head and proceeded to do as he'd demanded and fix her stepfather's food. Biting the inside of her cheek, contained any retorts she wanted to make.

"You really should wear more dresses," Travis said as he sat down at the small table. "It's not right that a girl your age wear jeans all the time."

"I like jeans." She began to heat some spaghetti sauce and put water on to boil. "They're comfortable."

"What about that dress I bought you? You should wear that," he continued ignoring her response. "I'm sure your mother would love to see you in it. You look so pretty in it."

A shiver of repulsion swept over Melissa as he spoke. She was thankful to have her back facing him as she made a face. Closing her eyes, she wished with all her heart that she could be anywhere else. Someplace where a grown man wouldn't look at her as though she were older than she was. Where she could go to her bedroom after school and have someone taking care of her, fixing her supper.

She felt a wave of horror at the traitorous thoughts. Having that meant she'd have to leave her mom. And Melissa knew her stepfather would never care for the frail woman. As long as her mother was still alive, Melissa would gladly stay there, hoping to make whatever time her mom had left as easy and peaceful as possible. If having a normal life meant she had to abandon her mother, she would prefer to put up with her stepfather.

"Spaghetti again?" Travis grumbled as she strained the noodles. At least her body had continued moving while her thoughts were far away.

She shrugged. "It's what we have."

"Then I suggest you go to the grocery store tomorrow. I'm not eating this shit again."

"I'll need some money." She handed him a plate of food.

"Here." He counted out and handed her five twenty dollar bills. "Don't forget to give me the change. And I better see a receipt. You're not going to waste it buying makeup or any of that other shit girls your age get."

"Yes sir." Melissa sat and took a bite of her food. She was so absorbed in her own thoughts she paid no attention when Travis stood. She only hoped he would go to the bar, as was his usual custom.

"You know, I think, you should get your hair cut." Her hair was pulled up tightly, forced back from her face. "Yeah, I think since you don't bother to actually fix it you should simply cut the shit off. I'm tired of seeing it always hanging down in your face." One of his hands moved to her neck as he stepped closer to her, practically pressing himself into her back. "Of course, I could always be persuaded to allow you to keep your hair…"

Melissa fell out of her chair in an attempt to get away from him. "I…I have to go s-study. Bi-big test tomorrow…"

She crawled backwards, away from him, turning and running into her bedroom as soon as she could.

Her back pressed against the door, Melissa's eyes were clenched shut as she kept her full weight braced on it as she prayed that he hadn't followed her. Within a few moments, she heard the front door slam shut, and released the breath she'd been holding. Peeking out the window, she saw her stepfather walking down the street.

She returned to the kitchen and fixed her mother some broth, taking the lukewarm liquid to her bedroom.

"Thank you, sweetheart. You do too much. It's me that should be taking care of you."

"I love you, Mommy," Melissa said, tears in her eyes. She wanted to tell her mother what was going on, to confide in her about how Travis was treating her. She knew if her mother wasn't sick that bastard would be out of their house in half a breath.

But the fact was, her mother was sick, and Melissa refused to add to her worries.

"I love you too, baby. I love you too."

Settling down beside her mother, she opened her book and began to read aloud once again.

CR&CO

Melissa sprang up, tears falling from her eyes. Scrambling out of her bed, she jerked on the closest pair of jeans she could find, panic filling her entire body when she didn't hear her stepfather's familiar snoring.

Sitting back down, she reached for the book bag she kept beside her bed at all times. She wanted to get a book out of it, so she could give the appearance of "studying" should he stick his head inside her door when he got back from the bar.

Groping around for the bag in the darkened room, she looked down, startled when she couldn't find it. Forcing herself to take several deep breaths, she wondered where she could have left it. Turning the light on, Melissa looked around the room.

Slowly, reality came back to her.

She was safe. She wasn't back in her childhood home and she didn't have to worry about Travis coming into her room. Gareth would kill him if the man came within five miles of her.

Leaving her room, she walked down the hallway and entered her bathroom. She immediately wet a washcloth with cold water and dragged it over her face. Looking at her reflection, at the tears still falling down her cheeks despite her ministrations, she shook her head.

It had been so long since the last time she'd had such a dream. She'd begun to wonder if maybe it was time to finally allow herself to believe she could be happy.

Passing her brother's room on her way to the kitchen, she knew he would be at La's place. He'd also be furious she didn't call him to tell him of her nightmare, but Melissa refused to ruin his day.

Looking at the clock, she noticed it was only four in the afternoon. Unable to go back to bed, to face more memories of her past, she heated some leftovers before returning to her room. She grabbed a clean shirt and tugged it on before quickly returning downstairs. Leaning on the counter, she began to chew the tasteless food.

Why now? Why did he have to try to come back into my life now? It's been twelve years. Twelve, all too short years.

But then you never really *expected me to give up did you?* She heard her stepfather's voice in her head, causing her to shiver. *No matter what Gareth said, you knew I'd never let you go.*

She shook her head. No, she hadn't believed he would give up. His pride had been too badly bruised by Gareth.

"I gotta get out of here," she said, pushing the food away. After grabbing her purse she practically ran out of the house, trying to escape the hated voice inside her head.

⋘⋙

"What happened last night?" Bram asked Duncan casually as he entered the control room. His body language belied the calm tone he was using. Bram was pissed.

"Nothing I couldn't handle."

"Duncan…"

"I handled it." Turning, Duncan looked at his boss. "Any word on that cutie you invited back to the club?"

14

"No. And don't think I didn't notice the fact that you changed the subject. Now, are you going to tell me what happened?"

"I'm not sure. I don't know the whole story."

"Damn it," Bram began.

"It's been handled. Damn, you know as well as I do that Melissa isn't a shit starter, so drop it."

"Mel? Yeah, she can get a pass. This once. Next time, she's out. I can't go around showing favoritism."

"Understood. Now, if you don't mind, I believe that hot new bartender you just hired is about to strip in the back room..." Duncan turned his attention back to the monitors as he watched the voluptuous blonde enter the room, as though on cue.

"I'm gonna make you start paying to have this room cleaned," Bram said, a mixture of humor and disgust in his voice. "Do you know how much I have to pay someone to get come out of the keyboards, off the walls?"

"Hey, I figure they all know about the cameras. So if they're gonna give me a show, I'm going to enjoy it."

"So what's your excuse when it comes to getting off with the patrons?"

"Someone has to watch them to make sure the situation is handled properly," he answered with a smile.

"You are such a freak." Bram chuckled a second before the door closed. Despite the words, Duncan knew the other man was teasing him when he used the term.

Turning his attention away from one of the few men he considered a friend, Duncan gave his full attention to the beauty on the screen.

As his cock hardened, he quickly unzipped his pants and spread them open before stroking himself as he watched the bartender begin to strip. As he'd explained moments ago to Bram, all of the employees knew about the cameras hidden throughout the club, so he didn't feel the least bit guilty about watching her, or jerking off to her little show.

Hell, if she didn't want people watching her, she'd change in the bathroom like everyone else does.

His strokes quickened, and he groaned when he saw the woman pinch her nipples with one hand as the other moved between her legs. With a groan, Duncan tried to catch all of his come in his hand. The last thing he wanted to hear that night was Bram bitching—again—because Duncan had to bring the mop in there. Again.

His eyes still on the screen, he saw the blonde's head fall back as she twitched from her own climax. Looking at the camera again, she blew him a kiss before she dressed.

CRBO

After entering Club Strigoi, Melissa was pulled immediately to the side by Bram.

"How are you doing tonight, Mel?"

"Fine," she lied. She couldn't seem to get her bastard stepfather out of her head. She could hear him taunting her, promising retribution for walking away from him, for injuring his pride and daring to think she could free herself from him. But he didn't need to know that. No one did.

"I know things got a bit…heated last night. We won't have a repeat of that will we?"

"You know me, Bram. I put a stop to shit, I don't start it."

He nodded. "That's good to hear. Have fun tonight and tell the bartender to give you a drink on the house."

Melissa laughed. "You know I don't drink." On impulse she kissed his cheek. "But thank you."

"Go have fun."

With a lie that she would do just that, she headed for the usual table, feeling anxious. She wasn't sure if she did or didn't want to see Gareth. On the one hand she wanted more than anything for him to wrap his arms around her and tell her everything would be fine, just like he'd done when she was younger. But on the other she didn't want to burden him. She didn't want to ruin his happiness by telling him her stepfather was trying to nose his way back into their lives.

All afternoon she'd been unable to concentrate. Every shadow seemed to have her stepfather's form, to be waiting patiently for her to be alone so he could jump out and grab her.

I'm not a baby, I can do this myself. I don't need him to fight my battles anymore. Her mind made up, Melissa was determined to not allow her past to intrude or to disrupt her brother's life again.

Approaching the table, she was relieved to see Diane was nowhere around. Mona, however, watched her very closely as she sat down.

"Are you going to tell me about it?"

"There isn't too much to tell."

"Not much to tell? I saw you last night, baby girl. *You* do not meltdown, Mel. I can't remember once ever seeing you lose control in the four years I've known you. You're the one that keeps Gareth from going nuclear. Last night I didn't think you were going to stop. I thought you were going to kill that woman."

"She just struck a nerve." Melissa shifted uncomfortably.

"I'm going to find out. You pulled me into that conversation and I deserve to know the truth. Now, do you want to tell me, or…" Mona's voice trailed off.

She didn't need her to finish the statement. Mona would find out whatever information she wanted to know, whether Melissa wanted her to or not.

"Please, just trust me. It won't happen again. I know what to watch out for, and I won't allow myself to lose control like that again." She looked deep into the other woman's eyes. "You know me, Mona. Trust me."

"I *thought* I knew you, Mel." She lifted her hand, moving it closer to Melissa's arm. At the last second, she shook her head. "A scratch, Mel. If I see as much as a single scratch caused by you on that woman, Diane, I won't stop next time."

Relief coursed through her body. "I won't touch her," she eagerly promised. The last thing she wanted was to see pity from yet another of her friends because they'd learned the truth about her. She got to see more than enough of that growing up and didn't think she could handle seeing those looks return.

Thankfully, her brother chose that moment to join them. Sitting beside her, Gareth put his arm around her shoulders. "Hey Mel, beautiful night don't you think?"

"Wow, you get laid and suddenly there's a whole new you. Remind me to send La some flowers for putting up with your ass," she teased.

Gareth's smile vanished as he looked at her. "What's wrong?"

"Nothing," she lied.

"Mel, don't you lie to me," he growled. "Did someone touch you? I'll kill him. Who was he?"

"It's nothing. I had a nightmare, that's all. It's really nothing," she tried to convince him. *Please gods, let him believe me and drop the subject.*

"Little Bit, why didn't you call me?" he asked, pulling her closer into a hug.

"Why, so you could burst into flames? No, I enjoy having my brother alive and walking around, not in an urn on my mantelpiece, thank you very much."

"Melissa..." he began to argue. It was never good when he used her full name. "You know I'll do it," he threatened.

Annoyance coursed through her. That was the only downside to having a vampire for a brother and a sorceress for a friend. They could essentially enter her mind whenever they chose.

That made twice in a single night someone had threatened to take a tour of her brain. One little meltdown and suddenly they acted like she was unstable.

"Then you're going to have to do it because as far as I'm concerned, nothing happened."

For a moment he looked as though he believed her, and she fought a sigh of relief at her bluff. Without giving her a chance to relax, he spoke. "You never look like this when there's nothing going on."

Before she could move, he had her finger in his mouth. Melissa felt his fang pierce the skin and hissed from the slight pain. Her eyes narrowed as he sucked on the digit then closed the wound. Pulling her hand back from him, she had never wanted to slap him so badly.

"That hurt," Melissa complained. She could feel him looking around inside her brain. She tried to shield the previous night's events from him, but she placed the walls up too late. He'd already seen what he wanted to know.

Eyes narrowed, Gareth ignored his sister and looked at Mona. "Where the fuck is she? I'm going to kill her with my bare hands," he growled.

"Who?"

"That bitch Diane." He began to stand, but Lalita arrived in time to stop him.

"What's going on?" she asked in a deceptively calm voice. "Leaving me so soon?" One look at Lalita's closed expression told Melissa all she needed to know. Her brother got the same look on his face when he was angry.

Looking back at Melissa, Gareth opened his mouth to say something. She knew he was going to tell La what was going on.

"No," Melissa screamed through their link. When his attention shifted to her, she continued, *"Please don't. I don't want everyone looking at me like that. I couldn't bear it if they knew... Please, Gareth, she's my friend. I don't want to see pity in her eyes whenever she looks at me."*

She could feel the tears welling, both in her eyes and in the link that bonded them, but made no move to wipe them away. She held his stare, praying he would understand.

She knew Lalita was his mate now, or close enough that it made no difference. Deceiving her would be wrong, but she just couldn't stand knowing that the other woman knew the horrible truth about her past.

"Gareth wants to kill Diane." Mona filled Lalita in while brother and sister stared at each other. "I'm not sure why, though."

"Why do you want to kill her? Not that I'd actually mind, per say, but I'd still like to know why," Lalita said, her voice still incredibly calm.

"She, um…" He hesitated. Melissa gave the barest shake of her head. "She insulted Mel last night."

"She did?" Mona's expression was stunned. "I'd have thought she would steer clear of her after—" She stopped in mid-sentence, quickly bringing her drink to her lips so she couldn't continue.

"She uh, met me outside. She didn't exactly like what I, um, *said* to her inside the club. We'll leave it at that. She had a right to feel that way, even if I wish she had chosen a different way of expressing it." Melissa shrugged, hoping they would accept her lie.

"O…K…" Lalita said, allowing the subject to drop. But it was clear from her tone, she wasn't satisfied with the answers she had gotten. Looking at Gareth she said, "Dance with me?"

"Next dance, I promise, La, baby. I want to have a chat with Mel first. I'll be out there soon."

Melissa didn't look back at her friend but assumed La must have agreed when she heard her working her way toward the floor.

"Mona, would you give us a—" Before he could finish, Mona stood.

"Why don't I just get us all some drinks." She looked at the pair and added, "I'll take my time."

When the other woman was no longer within hearing distance, Melissa asked, "So, how are things with La? You going to change her? Have you set a date yet? Do I get to be a bridesmaid? But I refuse to wear pink, though I don't think I have to worry about that with La. She seems more a dark purple kind of gal to me."

"Things are fine with La. Or they were until we got here," he added grumpily, a pointed look at her. "I don't need to change her. She's—well, let's just say we have a lot more in common than I thought we did."

Her eyes widened. Lalita was vampire? She'd have never suspected it considering the way the woman acted. Shrugging, she decided it didn't matter. She liked La because of who she was, weird quirks and all, not because the woman was human—or in this case vampire.

"And we haven't discussed marriage yet. Now, no more changing the subject," he told her in a no-nonsense tone. "You should have damn well called me the minute that bastard's name was mentioned."

"You'd just left with La, you were so happy..."

"I don't fucking care. Damn it Mel, how can I protect you if you don't tell me?"

"I don't need your protection," she screamed. Closing her eyes, she was thankful for the loud music the club played.

"Your nightmare was about him, wasn't it?" Gareth growled, eyes narrowing once again.

"You already know the answer to that. Why do you ask me questions when you just go inside my head for the answers anyway? What am I, in high school again? What's next? Are you going to ground me?"

"Yeah, I know the answer. But I didn't have to look inside your head to find it. It's all over you."

Melissa looked at him and snorted as she rolled her eyes.

"Don't believe me? Go look in a mirror, sis. There are bags under your eyes, you're wearing loose fitting clothes, and you're constantly looking over your shoulder. I remember perfectly, how things were when you first moved in with me. I remember being able to walk past your room at any time of night and schoolbooks were littered around you, the catnaps you took. I should have killed that bastard the night you came to live with me." His voice was filled with disgust for the man that was her stepfather.

"I'm glad you didn't," Melissa told him softly, placing her hand over his. If anyone else did this, Gareth would see it as flirting. He'd probably rip their hand off before a word was said. "You were my hero. You *are* my hero. I needed to be rescued from a monster, not think I had traded one demon for another. Though, I'm sure you know I'd have practically sold my soul to get

21

away." She ignored the tears that began to flow down her face. "I'm going to go. I don't care what you tell La, as long as you don't tell her about my past, not yet. Please, just give me time to adjust to her finding out about it first."

"I don't want you out there all alone. What if you see him?"

"You bit me remember? If I think I see so much as his shadow jump out at me, I'll be screaming for you," she said, a small smile on her face.

"No, you won't." He smiled sadly. "I know you're more stubborn than that. I know you can take care of yourself it's just, with him…"

"I know. But you can't protect me all the time. I promise, Gareth, if I need you, I'll yell."

"You won't worry about interrupting anything?"

"As long as you promise to be at least halfway dressed when you get there, I won't," she teased. Her voice sobered. "If I really need you, I'll call."

Gareth nodded. She knew him well enough to know he wasn't comfortable with allowing her to simply walk off into the dark night alone. He, more than any other, knew what hid in the darkness, in the shadows, waiting for her.

Leaving the table before he could change his mind, she took a detour through the club, pulling Lalita to the side.

"It's my fault Gareth can't answer all of your questions tonight. I promise, you'll get the answers, but not now, not yet. It's something I have to work through. He cares about you, please understand that he's only trying to protect me if he refuses to answer you." Melissa hated the vulnerability she knew shined in her eyes tonight. But she'd caused enough problems for her brother for one night. She could easily swallow her pride for him. There wasn't a single thing she would not do for him, if he asked it, and practically nothing she wouldn't do even if he didn't.

Lalita stared at her for a moment than accepted her explanation with a hug. "I trust you, Mel. I'll try to be patient."

"Thank you."

"But that doesn't mean I won't still make him sweat for it."

Walking away from her brother's mate, confident everything would be fine between the lovers, Melissa slowly left the club. Sticking to well lit streets, she walked through the entire night, alone but for her memories. As the sun rose on a bright new day, Melissa was grateful she had once again survived the darkness.

Chapter Two

"Damn, I'm horny," Duncan grumbled as he sat down in front of the monitors. After her little show in the back room, the busty bartender had begun to change in the bathroom. Not even Gareth and Lalita went into the back room to fuck anymore.

If not for a few video files he'd grabbed from the security discs and kept for his own personal use, he'd be ready to strangle someone. As it was, he was more than ready to feel a pair of warm legs wrapped around his waist as he thrust into a woman.

Calling one of the other bouncers up into the room to keep an eye on things, Duncan decided to scout things out in the club.

Passing through the crowd, his eyes scanned in every direction for that blonde Melissa had tried to knock unconscious. There'd been no sign of her since the incident, just over a week and a half ago. He continued surveying the room, looking for someone who could help him out for the night. He did not want another case of blue balls.

"Okay, this was definitely a mistake," he said, half under his breath, watching Gareth and Lalita grinding on the floor right in front of him. Of course, it didn't help that he knew exactly what it looked like when the two began to really fuck.

Lalita was hot, but not at all his type. She was just too—Duncan shook his head, unable to place his finger on what it was that made him only look at her as a friend.

A hand touched his arm, forcing him to stop watching the two vampires in heat. Duncan turned his head to the left when he felt a touch on his forearm. His gaze started at the small hand on his forearm and traveled up the peaches and cream arm to an angelic face.

Melissa. And damn she looks good enough to eat.

He wanted to feel her in his arms again. Hopefully this time she wouldn't be struggling to get out of his embrace to rip someone's hair out.

"Evening, Mel. How's tricks?"

She rolled her eyes but tilted her head to the side, indicating she wanted him to follow her off the floor. Cock flexing slightly inside his pants, he nodded.

"I wanted to thank you, for the other night. I would have done something I regretted if you hadn't stopped me."

"You're welcome." Taking a closer look, he noticed the bags under her eyes, smudges that not even her expertly applied makeup could conceal. Noticing his scrutiny, she looked away. "Are you sure—"

"Shit." Her eyes darted back to him. "I gotta leave."

Holding her arm before she could move away from him, Duncan followed her line of vision and saw the woman she attacked the previous week striding into the club.

"Why?" He was certain he knew the answer, but wanted to see if she'd admit the truth to him. Melissa had to leave because of her.

"Because, if I stay I'm going to hit her. I promised Gareth I wouldn't cause anymore trouble."

"So, where are we going then?"

"*We* aren't going anywhere, I'm leaving."

Duncan gave an easy smile. "We were in the middle of a conversation. Come on, I'll make sure you stay out of trouble. I'll buy you some lunch and we can finish our conversation."

"Our conversation was finished. I wanted to thank you. I did. See, end of conversation."

Sandy Lynn

"I'm not letting go of your arm until you agree to let me take you to lunch."

She tilted her head to the side. "Fine, tomorrow is perfect for me. Of course, since lunch happens at noon, I'd love to see how you manage that."

Leaning down to her ear he inhaled deeply, his eyes closing at the pleasant smell of soap and only a hint of makeup. No perfumes or sprays masked her scent.

"Then I guess you're just going to stay in this club until we finish talking."

"That's blackmail." She glared at him.

"Angel, I've been accused of much worse things. So, what's it going to be?"

Looking back and forth between him and the blonde, she finally agreed, through her teeth, "Lunch it is."

Guiding her to the door, making sure he didn't bruise her flesh with his grip, he nodded at Bram before exiting the club. They were a few yards down the street when Melissa spoke again.

"You know, you can let me go now. I'll keep my word."

Even though he didn't want to lose the minor contact with her, Duncan obeyed. He stopped and watched Melissa look behind them, as though she were afraid they were being followed. For a moment he wondered if Gareth would come kick the shit out of him for leaving with her.

But when he followed her gaze, he immediately hissed in pain as he felt her foot coming down full force on his own, then her fist making contact with his jaw.

His teeth lengthened and his eyes narrowed. Staring at Melissa, he watched her rub her knuckles and continue walking. An outside observer would never believe she'd just hit him. She gave no signs that anything had just happened, unless you saw one hand smoothing over the other.

"What the fuck was that for?" he shouted.

"I don't like being told what to do. Now, are you still buying me lunch, or am I free to go about my business?"

Shaking his head, a corner of his mouth twitched as he fought not to smile. "Nice punch."

"You damn near broke my knuckles," she complained, but after she looked at him, she appeared much more relaxed.

"If you don't like people telling you what to do, how does your brother get away with it?"

"He's different."

"That's pretty aggressive. I think I like it," Duncan teased her. He couldn't believe he'd never seen this side of her before. It was a side that excited him more than seeing Gareth and Lalita dancing. Her punch had his cock applauding, begging for more. With a chuckle he silently admitted, *I never said I wasn't a freak...*

She looked back at him, and blushed. "The foot thing was because I don't like being told what to do."

"And the right hook?"

"I don't like people pushing me around. I didn't appreciate you grabbing my arm and walking me away from Strigoi like I was a child."

Freezing for a moment, he was content to simply watch her walk. *A hellcat with the face of an angel. What did I do right so I know how to repeat it? And, does the hellcat attitude continue over into the bedroom?*

After a few steps, Melissa looked back at him. "What?"

Shaking his head, a huge smile on his face, Duncan chuckled. "There's more to you than meets the eye. Where'd you learn to punch like that?" He resumed walking, easily catching up to her.

"Gareth. He taught me how to defend myself."

"Your voice changes when you talk about him. You talk about him the way—" He broke off, unwilling to say anything else.

"What? The way what?"

Shaking his head, he continued the statement he'd tried not to say. "The way women talk about knights. Their voices get all soft, like they're in love or some shit like that. Like being back in time a few centuries, having some guy sweep them off their feet is their idea of true romance.

"And that is why I will never go watch one of those movies. Can't stand that dreamy tone women have afterwards." Duncan shook his head.

"What's so wrong with a woman wanting someone who will rescue her?"

"Nothing, I guess. But what they fail to realize is life wasn't actually like they show it in the movies. Chances were the knight that saved the day had ulterior motives. Someone was paying him, the reward the fair maiden would bestow, the reward the woman he was after would bestow; Doesn't matter who gave it, there was always a reward. And we won't even go into their bathing habits." Duncan gave a small shudder at the memory.

"Wow, I think you just managed to crush almost all of my youthful fantasies in five minutes. Besides, that's not the truth. I happen to know, for a fact, that there are honest to goodness noble men out there. Men who will rescue a 'damsel in distress' even though there's nothing in it for them."

"I see. And that's what all women want isn't it? A man that will rescue them?" Duncan shook his head. "I'll never understand it. Especially when they start screaming about being treated equally."

What does it matter what she's looking for? After all, it's not like I want more than one night with her. Well, maybe a few nights. He looked up and down her body.

"Maybe. But not me," she said, walking into the twenty-four hour diner.

◌წ◌

Melissa sat at an empty booth and forced a smile onto her face as she looked over the menu. The place was so similar to the one Gareth had taken her all those years ago on the night that forever changed her life.

"So what do you want?"

Duncan's voice brought her back to the present and for that she was grateful.

"Hmmm, their breakfast menu looks appetizing," she answered, deliberately misunderstanding the question.

"If you don't want a knight in shining armor, what do you want?" he repeated, being more specific.

"Honesty. I just want honesty. Why did you really bring me out to lunch?"

"You're sure you want the truth?"

"Yes." Pausing, she smiled at the waitress and ordered pancakes, bacon and hash browns with a large glass of orange juice. Duncan ordered bottled water.

She waited for the woman to leave before continuing. In the nearly empty building, they were almost assured privacy, but that was no reason to press their luck.

"Surprise me, tell me the truth."

"I'm horny." He shrugged, smiling as he sat, completely relaxed in the seat opposite her. "I was just looking for a piece of ass tonight." Before she could even respond to the chauvinistic comment, he held up a finger and continued. "I didn't plan on running into you, you approached me, remember? But, I can't say I'm disappointed."

"And you think after you feed me I'll feel...grateful?" Anger filled her. This was a trick she expected from high school boys, not him.

"Hell no. Actually, I was expecting a kick in the shin as soon as the word horny left my mouth."

Melissa couldn't help herself. She laughed at him. She'd told him she wanted honesty and he certainly didn't seem to be censoring himself for her sake.

"You're having problems sleeping. I just want to let you know that you can talk to someone."

"Why does everyone think I need to talk about my feelings?" Melissa almost shouted, her amusement and carefree attitude suddenly stripped from her. Closing her eyes she took several deep breaths.

"Angel, I know the look. There are skeletons in your closet. My guess is there's a few you don't want to tell brother dear about."

"And how would you know what that look is?" she demanded, done trying to keep an iron control on her anger. "And why in the name of the gods, do you think I would tell you anything that I wouldn't tell my own brother?"

Watching him closely Melissa wanted to growl when they were interrupted again. He smiled at the waitress as she set down Melissa's food. He waited long seconds that passed too slowly until she had stepped away before leaning on the table and addressing Melissa. "Because I've seen it. More in my life than you can imagine."

"You've got skeletons?" she asked skeptically, praying that someone really could understand how she felt.

Watching him as he took a deep drink from the bottle, Melissa sighed and began to eat, certain he wasn't going to answer her question.

"Skeletons, cadavers, even a maimed body part or two. You see, Angel, of all people, I know how much easier it can be to talk about your fears with a stranger than it is with your own family, or your friends."

"But we're not strangers," she protested between bites. "So what makes you think it'll be any easier for me to open up to you?"

"Aren't we? I may know your name and who your brother is, but that's all I know about you, except that you don't wear perfume and you're having problems sleeping. What do you know about me? My name? That I work at the club? Yeah, you know a hell of a lot about me. We're practically best friends."

Melissa looked up at him. He still gave the appearance of being as relaxed as when they sat down, but now she believed that was all a show.

He'd been nice to her and she'd done her best to drive him away. She'd punched him, halfway hoping he would swing back so she could justify not wanting to spend any time with him. Instead, he'd laughed and complimented her. He'd even basically told her he had stuff hidden in his past and she responded by being rude.

"It's hard," she told him, her eyes on her plate. "You go through the trouble to bury them deep, so deep that you're sure they can never see the light of day again… Even then you put locks and deadbolts and chains around the sections you hide them in. You force yourself to forget where you put the keys, how to get back to those memories, and still, as if by magick, they come back."

"I know exactly what you mean. This one time I tried to get rid of a sorcerer that pissed me off. I tied him up, handcuffed his hands behind his back, locked him in a trunk, chained it and threw it in the river. But the next night the bastard was back in the same bar, annoying the hell out of me."

Melissa froze, staring at him, a bite halfway to her mouth. "O-kay… What does that have to do with me?"

Duncan smiled at her as she finally began to chew. Reaching across the table, he wiped a drop of syrup from the corner of her lip then slipped his finger inside her mouth. Automatically, Melissa licked the syrup off him.

Pulling his finger from her mouth, he said, "Because it's the same principle. It does no good to bury someone, unless you strip them of their power first. Otherwise, they'll just keep popping up, annoying the hell out of you."

❧

When she was finished eating, he paid the bill and they walked out of the building.

"Tell me something personal about you," Melissa said, turning to walk backwards so she could look at Duncan.

"You mean the whole 'I committed attempted murder' story wasn't personal enough?" he teased, enjoying the way she had finally relaxed around him again.

"No. I want to know something personal. Something you wouldn't normally tell anyone."

"Okay, that rules out my hard-on." He laughed when she shoved him. "What? I'd tell any beautiful woman that was interested about that."

"I'm not... I don't want to be beautiful."

"Why? Tell me. It will make you feel better, Melissa. I promise, whatever you say will go no farther."

"Let's turn down this street," she said, turning left.

"What's wrong with going straight?"

"There's a light broken. Besides, I want to go left."

Looking down the street he saw the streetlight she was talking about. He'd have never noticed it if she hadn't pointed it out. Thinking back, he realized she had carefully kept to well-lit areas during their entire walk.

"I'm not going to attack you," he began, feeling offended. "I've never had to force myself on a woman yet. You're safe with me."

"Why do guys always say that? Is it supposed to be comforting? Macho? What? What makes you think you can protect me if I'm not even safe in the comfort of my own head?" She glared at him angrily.

"Who was he?" Duncan was pissed at how badly this poor sweet angel must have been hurt to feel such anger.

"No one. As far as I'm concerned, he doesn't exist."

Reluctantly he allowed the subject to drop. She wouldn't talk about it before she was ready, and forcing the issue would shut her down completely.

They continued walking in silence as the office buildings began to turn into elegant houses, the kind that boasted of owners with plenty of money and influence.

"This is my stop. I guess I should thank you for walking me home."

"Can I come in?" he asked.

"Still thinking about your dick?"

"No. Thinking about my flesh since the sky is turning pink. And well, I don't think I can get to another safe place before the sun is up."

Melissa blushed, and the gesture only made her more tempting to him.

"I didn't realize I'd kept you out all night. Yeah, sure, I'll show you to the guest room. Do you prefer upstairs or down?"

"I'm easy," he told her, unable to stop thinking about how much he'd love to see what her room looked like. "Where's your room?"

She shook her head. "No way, cowboy. That is not happening."

"Can you blame a guy for trying?"

"No. But it won't succeed."

Duncan followed Melissa through the house. She took him down to the basement, and a beautifully decorated spare bedroom.

"Sleep well, Duncan," she told him before leaving the room.

"Melissa?" he called out while the door was still ajar. "The offer to talk is always open."

She paused for a moment, then nodded once. "I'll think about it. Thank you."

Sighing, he began to slowly strip down to his boxers. He'd leave those on, but only because it wasn't his house.

At the memory of the bags under her eyes, the tension filling her body, he hoped she took him up on his offer soon. At the rate the poor girl was going, holding stuff inside like she was, Melissa was going to get herself into serious trouble.

CR&SO

Melissa paced around in her room, unable to stop thinking about what Duncan had said. She didn't want to talk about her stepfather. Ever. She'd bluntly refused therapy after Gareth rescued her. Now she wondered if maybe she should have gone.

No, she shook her head. *The therapist would have wanted to know all the details and I'd have been committed for thinking my "brother" was a "vampire".* Or worse, they'd have found out the truth and killed the only man who had ever meant something to her. The only man who had ever made her feel safe.

"I made the right decision then, and I'm making the right decision now," she told the empty room.

Walking to a corner of the room, Melissa carefully unfolded a circular rug and sat down in the center of it. With a deep breath, she cleared her thoughts, preparing to reinforce the barriers her brother had taught her to build to help shield her from thoughts of her stepfather.

The exercise was supposed to help guard her against the nightmares. And as far as she could tell, her stepfather was nothing more than one giant walking nightmare.

Her exercise completed, she took another deep breath then stood. Beside her bed, she stripped off her jeans, carefully placing them within easy reaching distance before she slid between the sheets.

Her hand poised to turn off the small lamp she had beside her bed, Melissa hesitated. Instead of completing the action, she pulled her hand away. Curling into a ball on her side, Melissa forced her mind to go blank before she drifted off to sleep.

♋♌

Travis stood outside, watching the house. He was so close to his goal, he just needed to be patient a little while longer. Then the little bitch would be his. He'd waited a long time to get revenge on her for what her and that freak had done to him. Lifting his hand to his neck, he wiped his hand across the spot where he'd been bitten. He'd never forget that night, the humiliation he'd suffered.

Patience, he counseled himself as the desire to just slip into the house grew. If she had been alone, he wouldn't hesitate. Hell, he would've made his move even if it had been that meddling fucker with her. Then he'd be able to catch them both at their most vulnerable. But he didn't know anything about this new guy.

After that little incident, he'd made sure to discover anything he could about vampires. People had laughed at him, called him crazy. His hand moved to the silver cross beneath his shirt. He'd learned how to protect himself from that stranger, but who knew what this new guy was.

The little whore, he sneered. Did she spread her legs for every man? Did she let that pointy-toothed bastard pimp her out? Rage filled him at the thought. She belonged to him.

A slow smile crept onto his face. Then again, at least now she'd be broken in. And he was positive they'd have taught her a trick or two. Things he'd be sure to take advantage of before he passed her around to his friends. He was sure they would pay for a taste of her. And he'd be sure she repaid him for every dime he'd spent tracking her down and that he'd had to pay that worthless bitch, Diane.

Not even she could do her job right. He'd hired her to lure the man away. She'd never mentioned any other men hanging around. She couldn't seem to do anything right. Perhaps he should make her earn her money another way...

Shaking his head, Travis decided to go back to his temporary home. The warehouse was perfect; no one would think to look for him there. And he needed to figure out how this new man could complicate things. The next time he called Diane, he'd tell her to discover more about him.

When he finally did get his revenge, he wanted it to be perfect. He had spent too long thinking about what he wanted to do to allow some new guy to fuck it up.

Walking away from the expensive house, he determined to return that night. So far she hadn't seemed to notice that he was following her. And he would continue to do so until the perfect moment arrived to strike.

Smirking, he knew she would never even suspect how close to her he was. She thought she was safe from him. And he would take pleasure in letting her know just how much of an illusion that was. She belonged to him, and he'd make sure she learned that lesson well.

Chapter Three

Looking down at the fresh grave, Melissa felt her heart break all over again. She'd never forgive herself for going to school that fateful day instead of staying at the hospital with her mother. She'd been inconsolable when she'd found out.

The principal, a typically nice older woman had come down to her class and Melissa could still hear her.

"Melissa, please grab your things and follow me to my office."

There had been the various calls and hoots from the other students, questions about what she could have possibly done wrong flew through her head, but she obeyed without question. Five minutes later, she was sitting in the principal's office, waiting to find out what she had done wrong, why she was in trouble.

"What's going on? Am I in trouble?"

"I'm so sorry to be the one that has to tell you this…" The principal knelt down in front of her. "It's about your mother."

"What's wrong with my mom? Did she have to get more tests? They said she was getting better." Melissa started panicking. "The doctors *said* she was getting better."

"Sweetie, the doctors were wrong. I guess your mom didn't want you to know how sick she was…she died. Just a little while ago."

"You're lying," Melissa shouted in the principal's face, shoving the other woman away from her as hard as she could. Without stopping to grab her books or her backpack, she ran to the door, tears flowing down her face. "You're a liar!" she screamed, and ran out of the door.

No one stopped her as she ran out of the school or down the street.

The only thought running through her head was, *She's lying. I don't know why she'd want to hurt me like that but she's lying, she has to be.*

She ran all the way to the hospital, ignoring the yells—the horns—as she ran full speed across streets disregarding any traffic, and even the burning in her side. All that mattered was that she got to her mother's side. That she see for herself everything was going to be all right. She'd tell her mother what that horrible old woman said, then, as she lay safely in her mom's arms, she'd get to hear her on the phone, screaming at the principal for trying to torture Melissa.

Pushing past the people leaving the hospital and shoving her way through the group getting off the elevator, she hit the button for her mother's floor repeatedly until the doors closed.

As soon as the elevator stopped, she was out of it, racing down the hallway, past the nurse's station and straight to her mom's room.

Melissa stared at the empty bed and tears began to flow down her cheeks.

One of the nurses must have seen her run into the room because she felt a pair of hands on her shoulders.

"She's just getting some tests run? Right?" Melissa pleaded, her voice trembling. "Right?" she demanded. "They just needed to run a few more tests before she gets to come home."

"I'm sorry," a gentle voice answered.

"But you said…the doctor *said* she was getting better."

"Your mother didn't want you to worry. She begged us not to tell you, she said she didn't want you sitting beside her bed, refusing to move. It was wrong, and I'm so sorry, but your mother didn't want you to live your life this last week as though the world had stopped turning. She didn't want you to stop living. She gave us this to give to you."

An envelope was pressed into her hands, but Melissa barely felt it even as her hand automatically closed around it.

A firm hand on her shoulder brought her back to the present.

"It's time to leave," Travis told her.

Melissa just shook her head. She'd never be ready to leave her mother. She wondered if her mom would have liked the dress she picked out for her to wear, or if she would have preferred the blue one. Her mom had always said the green was her favorite, but she'd only worn the blue one on special occasions.

When the hand at her shoulder grew more insistent, bruising her flesh, she had no choice. She still wasn't ready to leave, but she knew her mother wouldn't want people to see Travis dragging her through the cemetery.

Allowing him to lead her away from the fresh grave, she felt hollow inside. She felt completely numb to everything but the emptiness that now settled in her heart. It was as though she were somehow watching someone else's life unfold before her eyes.

When they reached the waiting car, her stepfather pressed the medicine into her hand. Mechanically, she took the pills.

Staring out the window as he drove her farther away from where her mother would rest for eternity, she wondered how the sun could possibly be shining on such a horrible day. Why wasn't it raining, why weren't the angels crying, like in that song her mother loved so much?

The next few days slid past in a blur. Her stepfather would give her medicine, and she would take it, feeling too dead inside to do anything but obey him.

A week had passed since her mother died and Melissa still spent her days curled around her mother's pillow, crying.

"You're not still crying are you? Damn, it's been a week, get over it already. The house needs to be cleaned and I'm hungry."

Ignoring him, she closed her eyes as she remembered how her mother used to read to her—before she got sick. She could almost hear the sweet voice, telling her a story. The words didn't matter. They wouldn't matter now.

The only thing Melissa wanted was to hear her mom's voice again.

When she felt the pillow being ripped from her hands, she opened her eyes and sat up on the bed.

"That got your attention, didn't it? Now get your ass up and fix me something to eat."

"Leave me alone," she said, snatching the pillow from him and pulling it close to her. Her body curled around it, protecting the item from him.

Without a word of warning, Melissa's face was thrown to the side, her cheek burning as though someone had just set fire to it.

"You want to cry so damn much, I'll give you something to cry about. This house better be clean when I get home, or so help me..." Travis didn't finish his threat. He didn't have to. Her cheek was already throbbing from his first blow.

She waited until the front door slammed shut before she left her room. As Melissa cleaned the house, her mind was far away, on a picnic she and her mother had enjoyed a few summers past. When she finished taking the trash to the curb, she went straight back to her room. Pulling the familiar textbooks out of her backpack, she littered them around her, in preparation of her stepfather's return home. She didn't want to give him any other excuses to come into her bedroom, to think that she had "free" time.

The next day at school, one of her teachers and the principal pulled her aside to find out about the large bruise on her cheek. Unemotionally, as though she were talking about someone else's life, she told them what happened. Shocked and outraged, they'd called both the police and her stepfather into the school.

Before her very eyes she saw him do a song and dance number.

Watching him, she hoped the group was too intelligent to actually believe what he was saying. Her stomach knotted as the other adults clung to his every word, every little detail he fed to them. By the time he was finished, he had everyone in the room convinced she was acting out to get attention.

Travis led her out of the school without so much as a harsh word. But when they got home, he slapped her face. Pain blossomed inside of her, but she didn't cry out, she didn't even whimper. She wouldn't give him the satisfaction.

"I better not *ever* get called back to your school. You made me miss half a day's work, you little bitch. Get your ass inside that kitchen and make me some supper."

Keeping her mouth shut, Melissa did as she was told.

In the weeks that followed, Melissa withdrew farther into herself. Whenever a teacher would look at her, or a friend would ask about her bruises, she would shrug and ignore them. She simply burrowed deeper and deeper inside of herself, hiding in the memories of a happier time, when her mother was still around to comfort and protect her.

⋘⋙

The first thing Melissa became aware of as she woke was the tears running down her face. That realization was quickly replaced by a man's arms around her.

Panicking, she struggled, trying to fight her way out of the embrace and unable to stop herself from screaming. Her struggles grew stronger when she felt the bare sheet slide over her legs.

"I need to study. I-I can't fail this test," she pleaded. When that didn't work she screamed, "Get off me." Her fingers curved and she slapped and scratched and kicked for all she was worth, her panic growing more acute when the arms around her grew tighter. Almost crazy with the need to escape this fate, she opened her mouth and began to scream, praying one of the neighbors would hear her. Uncaring of the punishment she would receive for the cops or some damn nosey neighbors interrupting Travis's plans, Melissa prayed for a small reprieve.

She prayed he would hit her hard enough that she would at least lose consciousness rather than be forced to endure his touch.

A hand went over her mouth and, even though she knew she would pay for the action later, her fear of what he was about to do was too much for her

41

to care. Clawing at the hand, trying to pull it away, she only managed to turn it slightly. Opening her mouth, she bit down on the hand as hard as she could.

A curse sounded through the room and one of her hands was pulled away, the motion much more gentle than anything she'd ever expected from her stepfather. A single finger was pried away from the rest, and Melissa wondered if he planned on breaking the digit as punishment for her bite.

Tears ran down her face and she whimpered, determined not to let him know just how bad he hurt her. Bracing herself for the pain, she was surprised when she felt her finger slide over his lips.

A shudder went through her body and she began to struggle again, harder. But his grip was firm. Her finger went between his lips and her entire body locked up as she felt the sharp fang. When her struggles eased, she heard a sigh.

"If I let you go, will you stop trying to rip me apart?"

A wave of relief swept over her, warming her blood from the cold panic that had washed through her. "Yes," she croaked. "My-my light…"

"I think the bulb blew," Duncan's voice came, followed by a clicking sound as he tried to turn the light on. "If you tell me where I can find them…"

"The closet. Just across from my room."

She heard him step away and took the time to quickly pull on the pair of the jeans she always had beside her bed. She had a feeling Duncan took more time than he really needed to get the bulb. That he was giving her the opportunity to collect herself.

By the time he came back in, she was dressed and feeling a bit more in control of her emotions. Melissa heard him unscrew one bulb and screw another in as she tried to figure out what to say. Brightness filled her room, allowing her to finally relax completely.

Looking at his scratched up face as he stood beside the bed, she felt guilty for having hurt him, even if the scratches were already beginning to heal.

"I'm so sorry," she began, turning her back and reaching for the hairbrush on her dresser, just to have something to do.

"I'll heal. Are you still going to tell me you aren't having any trouble sleeping?"

"Who are you, my brother?" she asked nastily, before she could curb her temper. "What the hell were you doing in my bedroom anyway?"

"I couldn't sleep. I got up to get a drink of water and I heard you cry out. Forgive me if I wanted to make sure you were all right. It was a mistake I won't make again." Duncan turned to leave the room.

"Thank you," she said quietly, staring down at the brush in her hand.

A quick glance at the door revealed Duncan looking back at her, his hand poised on the knob.

"Look, I know it's not easy to talk about shit when you wake up like that. But damn it, you need to talk to someone. If you refuse to talk to your own brother, and you won't talk to me, you need to find someone you *will* talk to before whatever you're running from destroys you." There was a pause. "I won't bother you again."

Looking up, she watched as he left the room.

Her fingers automatically braided her hair into one long plait down her back as her mind went back to the horrible dream. As much as she hated to admit it, he could be right. He at least deserved to know that she'd had a nightmare about her mother.

With slow steps, she exited her bedroom and went down to the kitchen. She grabbed two of Gareth's tall bottled waters from the fridge, then stuck her head inside the den and the living room before heading down to the guest room.

Knocking on the door, she waited a moment for Duncan to respond. When no response came, she knocked again. "Duncan, it's Melissa," she said, feeling a bit foolish. *Who else would it be, he knows Gareth isn't home.*

Waiting another minute with no response, she was turning away, assuming that he either really didn't want to talk to her, or he'd fallen asleep pretty quickly, when the door opened.

He waved her inside. "Come on in."

"Thank you. I thought you'd like some…" She handed him the water, trying not to notice that he was walking around in his boxers. "That's a pretty cool tattoo. I didn't know you guys could get tattoos. Gareth always said they wouldn't last, something about your bodies rejecting them."

"You have to use a special ink or it won't take." He lifted his hand to the claw marks forever ripping his flesh open. "A sorceress enchanted the ink for me. It isn't very easy to do—it uses a lot of magick—so, not many vamps have them."

Nodding as she opened her water, Melissa struggled to figure out what she should say.

"It was a nightmare," she began lamely. "I was dreaming about my childhood. About…" Her voice caught. "About my mother."

Remaining silent, Duncan allowed her to talk. He could feel the grief rolling off her as she sat down on the bed. He knew how hard it must be for her to open up, and he wouldn't rush her story.

"My mom died when I was fourteen. And life with my stepfather was…not easy." She looked across the room, anywhere but at him. "I was dreaming about the day she died. About how much my life changed."

He sensed her closing down. There was more to the story, but he had a feeling she wouldn't tell him what was going on if he didn't step in.

"I have trouble sleeping some days myself. I remember what I was like eighty years ago, and I'm not very proud of the things I did. I was a different person. I was the person people called if they had a 'problem' to take care of."

"That doesn't sound so horrible," Melissa said, before taking a sip from her bottle.

"I was an assassin, Melissa. Of course, sometimes people called on me to simply scare someone into cooperating. I wasn't a very nice man, and no one was ever happy to see me. Even the top crime bosses were afraid of me. I gave no man my allegiance, and all of them were terrified of the night I would turn on them. And they all knew, given the right price, I *would* turn on them."

"That sounds like a rough life. Feeling like no one wanted you around, no one cared. You could have just walked away—simply disappeared one night and no one would have ever thought twice about what happened to you."

"Tell me about it, Melissa," Duncan asked, his voice soothing.

"From the day my mother died until the night Gareth walked into my life, life wasn't worth living. My stepfather...he used to hit me—never when my mother was alive, but after..." Melissa's hand rose, cradling her cheek as though she'd just been hit.

"Did you tell anyone?"

She gave a cynical laugh and nodded. "Of course I did. I walked into school with my entire left cheek dark purple, clearly bruised. They pulled me into the office with that speech about how the principal was my friend, how if someone was hurting me I should tell them.

"Well, I told the principal what happened. But when they called Travis in, they believed him when he said that I was acting out. That I just wanted attention and wanted to leave him because I blamed him for my mom's death. That I'd do anything to make him look as though he weren't taking care of me. Of course they believed my stepfather. After all, I was just a stupid kid, right? I mean, after all I had just acted out a week earlier, shoving the principal when she told me my mother was dead. I shoved her and screamed in her face, calling her a liar, so of course it was easy to believe I was merely acting out. It was easier for them to remain in their safe little world than think that I could be getting hit."

Anger filled Duncan. He wanted to rip apart the people who had sworn to help Melissa if she confided in them, but turned her away when she asked for help. Unable to resist, he pulled her into his arms, the movement one of comfort and nothing else.

For the first time in a very long time, he held a beautiful woman in his arms and merely wanted to offer her his strength, his acceptance...his comfort.

"Tell me how you met Gareth," he asked softly.

Melissa pulled out of his grasp. "I ran away from home. My stepfather had gotten worse. He...he was going to...he wanted..."

Tears flowed down her cheeks and Duncan didn't need to be able to read her mind to know what her stepfather had wanted. Pure rage filled him at the thought, and he wanted the man's blood. He didn't even want to drink it, positive the blood of such a foul man would do nothing more than churn his stomach. But he did want to watch as the man died a slow, excruciating death.

It seemed as though now that she had begun confiding in him, she couldn't stop her story.

"But I ran away before he could do anything. I decided I'd rather sell my body on the street than let him... I'd rather have perfect strangers use me—let them do whatever they wanted—instead of spending another minute with him. I was so lucky," she said, shaking her head. "The first guy I tried to 'pick up' was Gareth. He took me to a diner and bought me something to eat.

"When he took me home, my stepfather slapped me, right in front of him. He didn't care that I had left, he cared that no one had been around to make his supper or clean his house. Gareth took one look at my stepfather and threw him across the room. He told him if I had so much as a scratch on me the following night when he came to pick me up, the man would pay dearly.

"That was the longest night and day of my life. I was terrified of what would happen if he didn't come back, what my stepfather would do to me. But I packed, just in case. I didn't have much I wanted to take with me, but there were a few special things, memories of my mom... And just like some kind of white knight, as soon as the sun set, he was there at the door, with papers that proclaimed he was my 'long lost brother'. My stepfather gladly signed custody over to him, when Gareth flashed his fangs again. When we left, he took me out to eat and bought me clothes. I felt like a princess that night.

"For the longest time I kept waiting for the other shoe to drop. For Gareth to tell me that I was going to become some kind of pet, an open buffet whenever he was hungry, and gods help me, I didn't care. I waited for him to tell me what I owed him for 'rescuing' me, but he never did. He always treated me as though I were really and truly his sister."

Duncan pulled Melissa into another hug. He wanted to tell her how sorry he was that she had been forced to go through that growing up, but words were meaningless. Her story went a long way to explain the close relationship between the brother and sister. It completely explained why the man was so over-protective of her and why, no matter what happened, Melissa stood beside her brother, unconditionally.

"How does that blonde figure into this?" Duncan asked.

"She's working for my stepfather." He felt her hot tears drip onto his chest, but she didn't try to pull away this time. "He's never forgotten how badly Gareth humiliated him, how he saved me. He wants to destroy my brother, Duncan. And all I can do is scream in the darkness, wait for him to grab me. I think I could handle anything he did to me," she told him, her voice muffled slightly. "But if he hurts Gareth...if he hurt Gareth, I would never forgive myself." Looking up at him with liquid brown eyes, she pleaded. "Don't tell him. Don't tell Gareth."

"Angel, I don't think I can keep something like this from him."

"He knows about the blonde. And he knows about the nightmares. But Gareth thinks I'm still afraid of him—of Travis. I don't want him to know what really terrifies me is the thought of him being hurt because of me. He'll think it means I don't believe he can 'beat' Travis. I don't want him rushing into a situation recklessly because he wants to prove something to me."

Duncan nodded. "I won't tell him." Pulling her closer to him, he couldn't help his body's reaction to her. "I have one question. It's a little personal, though."

"What?" She gave half a chuckle. "I've just confessed my deepest, darkest fears. What's one more answer?"

"Well, I know you stomp on a guy's foot for bossing you around, and you punch them in the jaw for pushing you around. What do you do if a man kisses you?"

His question took her completely by surprise. "Black eye," she answered automatically.

"It's definitely worth it," he said.

47

Sitting there with Duncan's arms wrapped around her, Melissa watched, spellbound, as he lowered his head to hers.

When their lips touched, her eyes drifted closed. She expected to feel his tongue inside her mouth, some kind of invasion, much like the other kisses she'd received. But he took his time, his warm lips pressing against hers, moving slowly, easing a response from her as they pushed her worries away.

Duncan pulled away from her, kissing the tip of her nose. Opening her eyes, Melissa saw a smile on his lips.

"Definitely worth it," he repeated.

But she had never felt less like hitting someone. She wanted to feel him kissing her again.

Not giving herself time to stop and think about what she was doing, Melissa wrapped her arms around his neck, brought his head back down to hers. A low moan escaped her throat when she felt his lips pressing against hers. Sucking his lower lip into her mouth she nibbled on it, another sound escaping her as Duncan pulled her closer to him, his erection pressing into her hip.

He cupped the back of her head, deepening the kiss, his tongue darting out to trace her lips. Her tongue moved tentatively, touching his. When he groaned, Melissa grew braver. She'd been kissed before, but never before had she ever felt so alive from the act.

It had always felt like more of a chore to get through. Thrusting her tongue inside Duncan's mouth, she began to play, learning his taste and reveling in the sensation moving from the pit of her stomach, down between her legs.

Her tongue moved inside of his mouth, exploring. When she felt the extended fang, her tongue pressed against it carefully.

He growled deep in his throat and shifted her so she was sitting on his lap. He leaned into the kiss, still allowing her complete control, as Melissa traced his lower lip.

Parting from her slightly, his mouth pressed against her cheek, trailing tiny kisses and nibbles to her ear. She turned her head giving him better access. Without quite remembering how she'd gotten there, she felt her cheek pressing against a pillow. When his mouth released her ear, she turned to look into his warm gray eyes. She didn't care how she had gotten in this position so long as he didn't stop.

Closing her eyes, she wondered how she could have ever thought of such things as a chore. How could she have never known just how great this felt?

"My beautiful angel," Duncan murmured before nibbling down to her throat.

Chapter Four

Duncan tried to control the lust raging inside of him. The last thing he wanted to do was take advantage of Melissa while her emotions were rioting within her. He thought he might have a grip on himself; that he might be able to let her get off the bed without ripping her clothes off.

But as he eased off her, she wrapped her legs around his waist and pulled him closer.

His mouth grew slightly rougher, his teeth nipping at her flesh, careful not to drink from her without permission. Duncan's hands went to her jeans in the scant space between them and unbuttoned the pants quickly. He pushed her shirt up with one hand, eager to feel her bare flesh arching against him.

His mouth trailed lower. A smile tilted his lips as he watched her enjoying his touch. Her eyes were closed and she was biting down on her lower lip, an expression of wonder on her face. If he didn't know any better, he'd think she'd never felt anything like this before.

A sudden thought crept into his mind. Did he know better? Had she ever felt like this before? Before he could ask the questions, Melissa opened her eyes.

"What's wrong?" she asked. "You stopped."

"Nothing's wrong, Angel. I was just admiring the view."

"Kiss me again?"

Leaning down to fulfill her request, he was amazed at how greedy she had become, how eager since the first kiss.

It was as though she couldn't get enough of him. His hand teased her nipple through the lace bra she wore. Shifting slightly away from her without breaking their kiss, he managed to free her breast from the barrier and continued to circle her nipple.

A moan escaped her and she arched her back, thrusting her breast closer to his hand. As he moved his hand, she whimpered. Balancing his weight on one arm, Duncan stroked the outside of her thigh, making gentle thrusts into her jean-covered sex. The action only seemed to make them both hotter.

Their kiss ended and, sitting up, he untangled her legs from around his waist. Carefully watching her reaction for any sign that she wanted him to stop, he saw her bite her lip. Her body writhed slightly, in an attempt to get closer to him. Tugging on her jeans, he tried to pull them away from her body so he could go back to tasting every inch of her flesh.

But as soon as the pants began to slide off her hips, her eyes jerked open and a look of terror destroyed any desire she had been feeling.

The once pliant, eager woman struggled against him, pushing him away. Scrambling off the bed, Melissa put her clothes to rights and stared at him, walking backwards until her back was against the wall.

"Melissa, what's wrong?"

At the sound of his voice she shook her head slightly. "I'm sorry, I-I think I should leave." Despite her words, her body remained stiffly against the wall.

Duncan stood then approached her slowly. Tilting his head, he noticed the flash of panic in her eyes and forced himself to take a deep breath. "Melissa, Angel, have you ever…" His voice trailed off. He was unwilling to embarrass her, but he needed to know.

"Have I ever what?"

"Have you ever had sex?"

Her eyes widened for a few seconds then narrowed. Pushing against his chest, she tried to move him away. "That is none of your damn business. Get away from me."

"Mel—"

"What?" she asked, still trying to push him away, but Duncan wouldn't allow her to run this time. Gathering her struggling body into his embrace, he tried to soothe her.

"Shhh, it's alright. Considering what you've been through it shouldn't be a surprise."

"Oh really? Are you sure you don't just want to call me frigid, like the other guys?" He felt her foot lift slightly and managed to move his before she stomped on it again. Keeping her arms tightly between them, he hoped she'd be unable to punch him again, either.

"No, Angel, I wouldn't ever call *you* frigid. The woman that I was just holding was anything but. It's okay to admit you're afraid of something." Duncan laid his cheek against her hair. "You can admit anything to me."

She began to struggle again, but just as quickly, the fight seemed to leave her. "It's not normal, *I'm* not normal. Guys have gone out of their way to make sure I knew that since high school."

"They were wrong." Backing up, his arms still wrapped tightly around her, he moved to the bed, pulling her down onto his lap when he sat down.

"A woman's first time should be special," he said, trying desperately not to trip over the words. "Damn, I wish I was better at this shit," he told her with a sigh. "It's something to be treasured and shit. Fuck, now I know why I was glad to be an only child."

"You seem to be doing just fine." Melissa giggled. "I'm sorry I freaked. I just…" She sighed. "The nightmares and remembering my childhood… The only time I was ever out of my jeans was when I was in the shower. And even then it was only for as long as absolutely necessary. I became mistress of the five minute shower."

"You can't be serious. Five minutes? That's, that's sacrilegious." Once again the desire to hurt her stepfather caused him to ball his hand into a fist as he tried to keep his tone light.

"So I learned," she told him, a smile in her voice.

"Mel, I won't ever do anything that you don't want me to do." All teasing left his voice. "If you want me to leave you alone and never touch you again, I will. If you just want me to hold you, I'd be happy to do that too."

She looked up at him, her expression disbelieving, but her eyes hopeful. "You'd be okay with that? What if I never wanted to...you know?"

"Angel, I won't ever force you to do anything. You have my word on that." Whether she realized it or not, his word wasn't given lightly. Once given, he would never break it.

After a moment of silence, Melissa nodded. "Will you just hold me? I don't want to be alone."

"Of course." Duncan stood up and paused, waiting for her to follow him. Pulling back the sheets, he climbed into the bed, holding them up for her to join him.

"You really don't mind?"

"I really don't mind."

She climbed into the bed and backed against him, making him force back a groan as her ass rubbed against his hard cock. He waited until she was settled before draping his arm over her waist.

Silence filled the room for several long moments as he tried to think about cold showers, some of the crime bosses he'd made hits for, his Aunt Martha, anything to keep from thinking about the beautiful woman in his arms and how badly he wanted her. Anything that would keep him from disappearing at dusk to go on a hunt, the kind he'd stayed away from for the last seventy-plus years since Bram had helped him change.

"Duncan?" Melissa asked, her tone betraying how tired she was.

"Yes, Angel?"

She mumbled something he couldn't quite make out. A few seconds later, her breathing was slow and steady, and he knew she was sleeping.

Lifting himself to his elbow carefully so he didn't disturb her, Duncan watched her. The fact that she had confided in him was enough for him to want to protect her. Hearing the cruel things that happened, the horrible names she was called by stupid boys trying to play at being men, was enough to make him want to hunt them down. But the blood he truly lusted for was her stepfather's.

The man had been given a great responsibility. Melissa and her mother had put their faith, their trust in him. For him to even attempt to do those things to Melissa was unforgivable. Duncan's blood raced through his veins as his temper threatened to boil over until he could no longer control it. His hunger grew as he thought of what he would like to do to the bastard who had treated the woman in his arms like trash.

Forcing himself to take a deep breath and calm down, he lay back against the pillow. His nose pressed against her neck, Duncan enjoyed her scent and the calming effect it had on his temper. Placing a gentle kiss to her silky flesh, he reluctantly stopped, despite her whimper. Beside him, Melissa tried to move back, pressing closer to him.

Eventually he was able to fall asleep.

෦෨෭

Stretching in the bed, Melissa felt well rested for the first time in over a week. She burrowed back against the man behind her, certain her brother had deliberately ignored her and come home to protect her. At that moment, she couldn't be angry with him, she hadn't felt so safe in a long time. Rubbing her cheek against the pillow, she sighed with contentment and debated about trying to go back to sleep.

Her eyes flew open when the hand resting against her stomach lifted to cup her breast. *What the fuck?*

A low moan came from behind her. Twisting her body around she felt a flood of relief when she caught a glimpse of gray eyes looking at her. The hand continued to knead her breast, but at least now she knew it who was doing it.

"I can't think of a better way to wake up," Duncan told her before pressing a whisper-soft kiss to her cheek.

"Do you mind?" Her face grew warm at the husky tone of her voice.

"Not at all." He smiled. "Okay, well, actually, since you mention it," he began, before pressing a kiss to her neck. Melissa felt his hand leave her breast and missed its weight. Before she had the chance to complain, she felt him glide under her shirt, over her bare stomach to cup her again. Now the only thing separating them was the thin lace of her bra.

His thumb skimmed over her nipple, causing her to press back against him, her eyes closing in pleasure.

"Much better."

"I thought you said you wouldn't force anything on me," she asked, more curious than complaining.

"I won't. Tell me to stop, and I will." He nipped at her neck and a moan of delight escaped her. When she didn't reply he removed his hand again, and she could feel him shifting behind her.

"You stopped," Melissa complained, opening her eyes.

With a slight chuckle, he smiled down at her. "Will you try something for me? I promise, if you don't like it, we can stop."

A shiver of fear swept through her body. Remembering how gentle and understanding he'd been earlier and looking over her shoulder into his warm eyes, she agreed.

Duncan nudged her until she was lying on her back then gently pulled her shirt up off her body. Fighting herself not to cover her body from his view, she lay there, wondering what he was doing.

"Your shirt is right here beside your head, Angel," he told her, easing some of her trepidation.

Nodding, she watched him, waiting to find out what he would do next. Lowering his mouth to hers, he pressed a gentle kiss to her lips as one hand stroked her arm.

"You okay?" Duncan pulled away slightly, still caressing her.

Melissa smiled. "Yes."

He lowered to her again, and this time she was ready for him. Wrapping her arms around his neck she pulled him closer still, licking his lip to encourage him to deepen the kiss. Groaning into her mouth, his tongue entered, rubbing against hers as he moved his hand over her stomach.

Melissa kissed him back as passionately as she could, her body pressed against him when his palm slid over her lace-covered breast.

Turning her head, she gave him better access to her flesh as he made his way across her cheek to her ear. She felt his elongated fangs slide over her, causing another shiver to course through her body, one that had nothing to do with fear. He gently massaged her breast, his thumb circling her nipple until it pebbled beneath his touch.

So many sensations filled her. Warmth pooled deep inside her, gathering until it centered between her legs, making her want to squirm beneath him.

His teeth grazed against her shoulder and she whimpered as his mouth continued to move lower. He eased the bra strap down her shoulder and shifted slightly. Looking down, she saw him watching her for any sign of distress as his tongue traced the swell beneath his lips.

He moved so slowly she wanted to cry out when he finally reached her nipple. Duncan laved it then blew gently across the wet area, causing her to arch up. Her left knee bent, she pushed against the bed, wanting to feel more of him.

Her hands twisted in his hair and Melissa closed her eyes, allowing the sensations to devour her.

How could this be happening? Never before had she ever wanted a man to touch her. Not since high school had she felt the slightest desire to be lying half-naked under a man as he set her blood on fire. She'd given up hope that someone would ever make her feel this way.

Above her, Duncan shifted his weight slightly and she could feel his knee pressing intimately between her legs. He teased her with his mouth until she was ready to scream, careful to show equally lavish attention to her other nipple.

Melissa could feel the erection pressing against her through his boxers and she felt a rush of pride. She had done that to him.

Urging him back up to her mouth, hands still twisted in his hair, she wrapped her leg around his waist. With minimal shifting of her position, she managed to free her other leg, allowing it to surround him, pulling him closer against her. Her lower body arched against him as his tongue delved into her mouth.

Again he traveled to the side of her neck, nipping her flesh. As his teeth slid over the sensitive spot just above her shoulder, she wondered if he would drink from her.

Did she care?

Hell no. Not as long as he kept rubbing her the way he was.

Duncan thrust into her jean-covered sex. Her pants and his boxers preventing anything from going too far, but the sensation of him rubbing his hard cock so intimately against her had her quickly moaning.

"Angel," he murmured next to her shoulder before once again taking her nipple into his mouth, tugging it with his teeth as he rolled the other between his thumb and forefinger. His knee pressed between her legs again when he lifted slightly, straddling her leg. Her hips arched forcefully and Melissa forgot how to breathe as she felt her entire body tensing. His leg pressed harder against her as she ground her sex into it, relishing the sensations that were being created.

Her fingers curled, pressing his mouth closer to her flesh. Her breath came in short pants as the pressure built between her legs. Her eyes squeezed tightly shut, and a scream tore from her throat as her entire body shattered around her.

Gasping for air, Melissa felt Duncan slowly release her nipple before resting his head against her breast.

"Gods," she whispered, unwilling to break the magick that seemed to surround them at the moment. Her first orgasm. It had felt better than any description she'd ever read led her to believe it would.

She felt him smile against her. "Did you like it?"

Did she like it? Did she like it! The term "like" did not begin to describe how she felt.

Duncan lifted his head from her and she could hear the concern in his voice. "Melissa?"

Nodding, she wished her heart would stop pounding so ferociously in her chest.

"I'm glad," Duncan said before lowering his head again.

She could still feel the erection pressing against her thigh, and wondered why he hadn't asked her for a similar release yet.

Or, was he just biding his time, hoping she would offer out of guilt? She hoped that wasn't the case.

CRBO

Rolling off of her was harder than he'd thought it would be. His cock strained inside of his boxers, begging for relief.

"I can, uh, help you out if you'd like," Melissa offered. A quick glance at her as he sat up told him she was uneasy with the thought. Grabbing his jeans and closing his eyes, he willed his body to cool as he stood, shaking his head.

"I don't want anything in return, Mel," he told her, forcing his jeans over his hips. Sitting beside her, he pulled her back into his arms, his mouth watering again at the sight of her exposed breasts. His cock twitched against the stiff fabric. "I didn't do that for you to feel obligated. I'm just glad you enjoyed it." He placed a gentle, chaste kiss on her nose.

"It just doesn't feel right to know you're still—"

He cut her off with a kiss. When he pulled back, he could see desire warming her brown eyes. "Angel, trust me, it felt very right."

Melissa blushed and looked away from him. "You don't want me to…"

Gripping her chin gently, Duncan turned her head until she once more looked in his eyes. "I really do. But that's not why I kissed you, Mel. That's not why I…" He smiled. "Angel, there isn't any rush to do anything."

"I'm not some innocent teenager you know," she told him, her voice sulky.

"I'm not saying you are. I told you before, I suck at this kind of reassuring shit. But don't rush things. I can't remember the last time I was with a woman who reacted the way you did. You gave me something special today, I won't ruin it by letting you do something you really don't want to do."

"Who said I don't really want to?"

Pulling her into his lap, Duncan allowed his fingers to linger on her flesh as he adjusted her bra. He kissed the swell of each breast before pulling her shirt over her head, hiding the tempting flesh.

"I can feel you want me to," she told him, squirming on his lap.

"You won't ever hear me say I don't want to fu—have sex with you. Small steps, Angel."

She looked at him, pain in her eyes. Did she think he wouldn't want to see her again if she didn't return the favor? He fought back a growl, adding the boys she had dated to his list of potential victims. He wouldn't kill them; he'd only beat them black and blue for scarring her.

"I'm not going anywhere, Angel."

"Yes you are. You're gonna go and fuck some woman that isn't an uptight little bitch." She tried to climb off his lap but he held her still. Melissa turned her face away from him, her voice angry as she spoke. "Let me go now, damn it."

"No."

"I'll punch you, I swear I will," she told him, looking at him again with her eyes narrowed. But that didn't hide the glimmer he saw in them.

"I don't doubt that, Mel. But I'm not letting you go." He didn't stop her when she balled her fist up.

"I'm not going to warn you again."

"I'm not letting you go."

Her hand flew out so fast even his predatory eyes could barely follow it until it connected with his eye. Growling he twisted, pressing her back against the bed. Restraining her hands, he made no move to stop her legs from kicking.

She fought against him like a woman possessed. "I'm. Not. Letting. You. Go. Damn it Melissa, listen to me. I'm not letting you go." She went completely still, her eyes closed and breathing shallow. "I'm not going to find some other woman to fuck."

She opened her eyes.

"I suck at this shit," he almost yelled. "Look, I'd really like to see you again. So unless *you* tell me you don't want that, I'm going to assume we have something between us."

"You still want to see me? Even after I punched you? Again."

"Yes."

"But what about…" Her voice trailed off.

"Well, Angel, as long as you don't consider Mistress Thumb and her four closest friends as cheating, I'll be fine."

"Duncan, I can't ask you to go without—"

He silenced her with a kiss.

"Mel, you didn't ask."

"I know about you. You're the kind of man that has a different woman every other night if he wants."

"Yeah, so? You're different. I never promised any of those women anything other than a night in bed."

"So what exactly are you promising me?"

"I'm not sure. I'll be there to listen to you, if you ever need to talk."

"My brother does that." She smiled playfully.

Releasing her hands, he arched an eyebrow. "How about this, I promise to kiss you senseless," he teased. Growing serious he continued, "Mel, I'm not sure exactly what to promise you, but I promise as long as we're figuring it out, I won't touch another woman. I promise to always be honest with you, and I promise I will be there if you need me, no matter who I have to go through to get there."

"Duncan…" Melissa shook her head. "That's so much to ask for from you. Especially when you aren't getting anything in return."

"That's where you're wrong. I'm getting everything in return." He silenced her blossoming protest with a kiss, his tongue easily delving into her mouth, delighting in her taste as she squirmed beneath him.

When the kiss ended, he climbed awkwardly off the bed then helped her up.

"I have one more question," she asked him, standing beside him.

"Yes?" He nibbled on her neck.

"What are we going to tell my brother?"

Duncan felt as though he had just been thrown into a lake in the middle of winter—in Alaska. His cock suddenly lost all motivation, as he remembered Gareth's reaction to the last man who tried to manhandle Mel on the dance floor.

Chapter Five

Sitting in the control room, Duncan wondered what he'd gotten himself into. He hadn't seen Melissa the past couple of nights and was wondering if he'd spoken before he'd thought the other night. It wasn't that he didn't want to be closer to Mel, that he wasn't attracted to her.

But a man like me doesn't have friends… And just forget about winning the lady like they portray in those movies.

He could remember seeing one particular movie about an ex-gangster with a soft heart. The man refused to kill his neighbor, instead becoming fast friends with the man. He didn't even kill the neighbor when the man learned his real identity and could expose him. Instead, the former killer went out of his way to help the neighbor live happily ever after while meeting his own perfect girl.

Real life was nothing like the movies.

Back when he was an assassin, it hadn't mattered how nice a person was, if they were the target, or they tried to stand in his way, they were as good as dead. It was one reason people learned not to fuck with him.

For the first time in years, he thought about the sorcerer he'd told Melissa about. He had a feeling she didn't believe he'd tried to kill the man. Stabbing him probably would have been a better method, but after the sorcerer pissed Duncan off, he'd wanted the man to suffer. Duncan had felt that slowly suffocating, or drowning, would be painful enough. It would give the sorcerer enough time to appreciate just how fucked he was.

Just as he'd told Mel, he'd completely bound the man. Tying his arms against his body then his feet together, he'd even handcuffed him just to be sure he wouldn't get his hands free. Dumping the sorcerer into a moderate-sized trunk, Duncan not only locked it, but he'd broken the key off inside of it, to assure no one would be able to get it open. And, just like in those corny cartoons they show on television, he wrapped a chain around the top, but that was to give it additional weight so it would sink quicker rather than additional security. But none of it had worked.

Giving in to the rare impulse, Duncan allowed himself to remember the past.

Walking into the bar, he saw the bastard sitting—alive and well—on a barstool and grew livid. Everyone around him quickly stepped away.

"Surprised to see me?" the sorcerer asked.

"What the hell are you still doing alive. When I kill someone, they die."

"Really? Then I guess you didn't do a very good job of it last night then," he taunted.

Curiosity filled Duncan. "How could you possibly have survived?"

Laughing, the man bought him a drink. Careful not to let anyone see he wasn't actually drinking the foul-smelling liquid, Duncan waited for an answer. He could be very patient when he wanted to be.

"It's all about power," the sorcerer said after a short time. "And between you and me, I have all the power in this relationship."

"Then this time I'll make sure to have the proper spells cast first," Duncan growled.

"It wouldn't hurt. But I'd still have all the power." The man's tone was so blasé; they could have been discussing the weather rather than his death.

"Explain it to me," Duncan said, his annoyance showing clearly through his gritted teeth and balled fist.

The sorcerer chuckled. "I annoy you. You've given me the power to annoy you. Why? And be honest."

Sandy Lynn

"I don't like bastards that think they can do whatever they want. That woman you harassed last night, she's a good woman. She's got kids. She needs her job and you almost made her lose it."

"So you're not made of stone after all. What's it to you? You're an assassin, a hit man. You kill people for a living. Don't you think it's a bit hypocritical? After all, you frequently do whatever you want.

"Unless... What does she mean to you? I've seen the way she looks at you, she's terrified of you. Everyone in here is."

"Everyone but you, it seems."

"So it seems," the sorcerer answered with a smile.

Duncan knew the man was right. She was terrified of him. Everyone who saw him was. And he frequently did get to do whatever he wanted because of that. He liked it that way. He enjoyed having none question him. But for some reason he wanted to tell her she had nothing to fear from him, he wanted to help her, to be a hero once in his life, even if only just to one person. But if anyone ever discovered he wanted to help her, neither the woman nor her children would stand a chance. He might as well kill them himself.

Shrugging, Duncan answered his question. "She's nice to me. She doesn't let her fear stop her from being polite, unlike most people."

"And that's why I have power over you. A man in your position can't afford to like anyone. Not if you plan on keeping your edge. Even now you're mad at me, yet you don't attack. Oh I can feel your desire to rip my throat out, yet you're talking to me.

"If you really want to kill me you have to take away my power first."

"I won't make the same mistake twice, sorcerer," Duncan growled, allowing his temper to reign.

"Good, good." The man nodded, taking a sip of his drink as though Duncan hadn't just told him he was going to kill him. "By the way, the name is Thomas." He took another sip of his drink then looked over at Duncan with a smirk. "Just make sure you strip all of my power, boy."

64

Duncan growled. "I won't forget. There's a powerful sorceress that owes me a favor or two. I'm sure she'll do the necessary spells for me."

Thomas laughed. "You're still not getting it. Let's try this one more time, a bit slower." Duncan bared his teeth in anger, but it didn't faze the sorcerer. "It does not matter if you strip my magicks or even if you kill me, I will still have power over you. So long as I have the power to annoy you, I will have power over you. At night, you'll hear my voice taunting you whenever someone makes you angry."

He turned to face Duncan. "You'll see my face when you kill them. You'll kill me more than once, you'll kill me every time your emotions run hot, every time someone annoys you. But I will always come back."

Staring at the man, Duncan thought about his words. When the bartender returned during a lull in their conversation, Duncan ordered the man a drink.

With a laugh, Thomas lifted his glass in salute. "That is certainly a good, if surprising, start."

Shaking his head, Duncan returned to the present. Thomas had been a good man. Unfortunately, he never concerned himself with who he pissed off.

A few months later Duncan had been hired to kill Thomas. Though, to be honest he'd wondered more than once if his death was ordered to test Duncan's fortitude. He suspected rumors had gotten out about the man he spoke with and, whether it was admitted or not, his friendship was the real reason behind the bounty on the man's head.

To his credit, Thomas never flinched when Duncan showed up to end his life. He didn't even seem surprised.

The man's final words still echoed inside his head.

"Do I still anger you, annoy you?"

"No," Duncan replied truthfully, stepping closer.

Sandy Lynn

"Then you've succeeded in removing my power over you." Thomas lifted his hands to defend himself with a spell. *"I consider you a friend, but that does not mean I will roll over and allow you to kill me."*

"I don't have any friends," Duncan responded coldly, a small piece of his soul was screaming, but he ignored it. *"But you have my respect. Because of that, I promise it will be painless."* Speeding up, he quickly moved behind the other man. Before Thomas could say another word Duncan grasped the man's head in his hands and quickly twisted it, snapping his neck.

Releasing him, he watched his friend fall to the floor.

"I can't afford to have any friends. But that doesn't mean I have to make you suffer either." Still looking at the body crumpled on the floor, he added, *"And if Tony doesn't like it, he can tell me so himself."*

Looking into the shadows, he stared at the almost invisible spy, sent by the boss to ensure he killed Thomas.

"While you're at it, tell him he's damn lucky I don't rip his eyes out for sending anyone to spy on me." Growling he spit out, *"Leave, before I decide I'm not feeling quite so generous."*

The boy scurried out of sight without hesitation.

Walking over to the sorcerer's cabinets he rummaged around until he found what he was looking for. Grabbing a bottle of wine, he opened it, and sniffed, quickly flinching away from the vile smell. Unlike humans, he knew exactly what would happen if he drank as little as one sip of the brew. Just how sick it would make him. But at the moment he didn't care.

With just a single sip of the vile liquid, he was ensuring that he would become deathly sick. It may not kill him, but he knew he'd wish for death. Unlike humans, his kind could feel the poison and rejected it quickly in an attempt at preservation. But right now he didn't care about the pain. He'd risk it for even just a few minutes of the forgetfulness that humans found in the alcohol.

Placing the bottle against his lips and tilting it, he drank deeply, shuddering with the taste.

Striding out of the man's house, he went to the house of a nearby sorceress that he kept as an occasional lover.

66

"What are you drinking, lover? Do you know—"

"I know exactly what I'm doing," he told her in a tone he knew would stop the questions.

"If you wanted comfort you could have just come straight to Peg. I'll take good care of you, I always do."

Removing his pants without his assistance, Peg teased his body as he finished off the bottle of vile liquid. He wondered if it would bring the blissful numbness that it gave humans. And how long he would have to wait before it took effect.

When he was undressed, she pushed him onto the bed, handcuffing him to the frame. Removing a fat candle from a drawer beside the bed, she lit it.

"Would you like to talk about it?" she asked before biting his stomach.

"No."

Wisely she allowed the subject to drop. Nothing she did, however, was able to distract him. He didn't even enjoy it the way he usually did when she drizzled melted wax on his chest and stomach.

Not letting her know he wasn't into their play, he mechanically drew moans from her as he thrust into her body. He didn't find release, but that was no reason to neglect her.

When she collapsed on top of him, completely sated, he looked up at the ceiling.

"That was amazing." She sighed. "I love it when you come to see me."

"Peg, I want you to do something for me."

"Name it, lover. Should I pull out the whips?" she purred.

"I want you to enchant some ink for me. I want a tattoo and I don't want it to ever disappear."

She sat up, still straddling him. "Do you know how much magicks that will require?" she exclaimed.

"A better question would be do I care. No, I don't."

"And if I refuse to do it?" she replied angrily.

"Then when I walk out that door we're done. And I'll make certain everyone knows we're finished." He didn't even raise his voice, but she blanched like he'd just slapped her.

She knew the only reason she hadn't been hurt was people knew she and Duncan were lovers. None made the mistake of thinking he loved her. But the last time an angry vampire had threatened her, she'd spread around that she was his favorite lover. Everyone knew he wouldn't be hurt by her loss, but she'd made sure they would think he'd be pissed.

"It'll take me about a week to prepare the proper spells..."

"Fine, now get these damn handcuffs off of me before I break your bed."

The second the restraints were off, he was leaning over her trash can, throwing up.

His hand covered the tattoo etched into his skin, hidden for now beneath his shirt. His relationship with Peg had ended soon after the design was completed. She'd been horrified when she saw the claw marks ripping through his skin, but he didn't care.

The picture was not for her. It was his final lesson from Thomas. One he'd allowed himself to forget, for a while. In his line of work he couldn't have friends. They were a weakness he couldn't afford. They made him vulnerable, open for attack. They were made targets—if only to find out if he'd become soft. A way to get revenge on him, the only way they could ever truly hurt him.

Every time he saw the bloody claw marks he'd been reminded of the pain being close to others caused.

Melissa didn't seem to mind the design of his tattoo much.

The thought of her brought a smile to his face. But it faded when he thought about what she'd been through. No one should have to suffer as much as she had, and he had a strong feeling she hadn't even told him the entire story. He would never blame her for not baring her entire soul. To do so left a person completely vulnerable. It opened them up to a pain that made torture look pleasant, and could easily rob someone of their soul.

Remembering his own past made him protective of her. Being forced to kill his friend and being abused by those who swore to protect you weren't truly the same, but they did infect a person with similar feelings.

No one should have to feel as though they had to walk the earth suffering in silence and feeling that they couldn't afford to allow anyone close to them without risking that person's life and happiness.

For years Duncan had refused to get close to anyone, refused to go through the pain that killing Thomas had caused, again. Though no one ever knew how badly that particular job had hurt him, the truth was, he'd never been the same afterwards. Not until Bram entered his life.

For some reason the stubborn vampire decided Duncan shouldn't have to be a loner, and befriended him. Bram had ignored his rudeness, his threats, until Duncan finally allowed himself to consider him a friend. Chuckling, Duncan remembered it had taken Bram over ten years but he'd never given up. He never pried into his past more than Duncan was willing to discuss, and he was the only person who was still living to know most of it.

It was thanks to Bram that the symbolism of Duncan's tattoo had evolved into a something different, something less bleak. Instead of forever remaining a reminder that he couldn't be close to anyone, it became a reminder of his past.

He had never regretted getting the tattoo, and just as quickly discovered he could never regret who he was. To dwell on the past, on the cold-hearted bastard he'd been was the road to madness. Plagued by guilt he would also be plagued with images of his victims, though none of them could ever be termed innocent. Too many faces to count, to remember, his guilt would quickly push him into insanity.

No, he could never be the kind of person who regretted taking another's life, could never regret what he'd done. He was the man he was today because of the man he was so long ago. Even then, Duncan had lived by his own code, refusing to break it. Any who tried to challenge his code were destroyed. He may not have been the best person, the nicest or most gentle man that lived, but he was an honorable man—as much as any assassin could be honorable. His only rule, the only hits he absolutely refused, involved children. In his long life, he'd never claimed the life of an innocent child. He did, however, kill more than a few of his fellow hit men until the gangsters learned the death of children was not something he would permit. If he even knew about it, the job was not completed. The criminals eventually learned to use different methods of torture to "persuade" a person to become compliant.

Looking at the monitors, watching Bram stand on the floor with his arms crossed, he wished his friend would find the happiness he truly deserved. He was the first man Duncan had ever truly called friend, and the only man he would ever stay truly loyal to. Thomas was the closest he'd had to a friend while he was a killer, but Bram was the one who helped him to walk away from his former life before the bosses could all combine their efforts in their desire to get rid of him.

They would have banded together—for a short while—to kill him. They were terrified that some night he would be at their door; a night on which he had not been summoned.

Bram was the man who showed him there could be more to life, and finally given him hope.

Watching his friend in the monitors, he hoped that the pretty brunette he'd seen talking to Bram would return. He'd only been able to get a glimpse of her the night she was in the club, but it had been enough to know that his friend was interested in her. If it could be more, no one would know unless she came back.

When Bram had told everyone on the staff to let her in the club and find him immediately, Duncan had decided to investigate. Going to the security cameras, he watched their encounter then managed to get a picture of her printed from the footage. Duncan gave the printout to Bram, who then made sure all the bouncers were shown exactly who to look for.

Retreating from the memories, Duncan watched the monitors for any sign of trouble. When Melissa entered, his eyes were drawn directly to her.

Could there be more between them than just the urge for him to help her? It had certainly felt like more when he'd held her. Why else would he have promised not to touch another woman so long as they were figuring out what was between them?

It was true, he enjoyed jerking off as much as the next guy—hell some would probably say he enjoyed it even more. But his hand was no substitute to feeling a woman's warm, wet pussy sliding down his dick. Just the thought of it, the memory of his cock thrusting in and out of a woman was enough to get him hard. He became uncomfortably harder when that woman's anonymous face became Melissa's sweet one.

On the monitor, she seemed to be looking for someone. Could he hope that it was him? Or perhaps she had changed her mind about ever seeing him again. That seemed more likely; she was looking for him to say she didn't want to see him again.

The gods knew it would be the better choice for her.

Giving in to temptation, he left the monitors, going downstairs with the intentions of ending things with Melissa before they went too far. He wasn't the man she deserved, he never could be.

"Go watch the monitors," he told the first bouncer he saw. When the man hesitated, Duncan rolled his eyes. "It's safe enough."

Damn, a man jerks off one or two—dozen—times and suddenly you gotta tell them if it's even safe to go in the room.

Staying back, he waited until Gareth left the table to dance with Lalita, thankful his cock softened enough to allow him to walk without a limp.

He didn't feel up to a confrontation with the man, and knew Melissa would be upset if he hit her brother. And he doubted she would care who swung the first blow.

Bram wouldn't be too happy either if an incident happened in the middle of his club.

Carefully, he approached her, keeping a lazy eye on the dancing couple, so he wouldn't be taken by surprise if her brother suddenly appeared.

Drawing closer, he watched Melissa at the table, talking with another woman. He knew they were friends, he'd seen them hanging out at the club together but couldn't remember the other woman's name. Her short, auburn hair was styled in a way that gave her the appearance of being sweet and innocent.

Anyone who had ever been around magicks would know better. The woman's power practically sparked as it flowed off of her.

Sandy Lynn

"Of course I think it's cute," Melissa told her friend. "Mona, I swear you are one of the few people that I think can pull off that hairstyle. And no, teenagers don't count. Seriously, you look fabulous."

"I'm just worried that now guys will think... Hello."

"Hey." He smiled at them, the forced smile turning genuine when he glanced at Melissa.

"Hey," she answered shyly. After a few seconds, she shook her head. "Mona, this is Duncan, he's a bouncer here. Duncan this is a good friend of mine, Mona. Mona's a—"

"I know. I can see the power surrounding her. Pleased to meet you, Mona." He offered his hand.

"It's a pleasure to meet you." She shook his hand, an approving expression on her face. "Not many people would shake my hand, knowing what you do."

"Duncan's not like most people," Melissa said then blushed.

"Well, I think I'm going to go...do something else. That way if Gareth asks me what's going on, I can honestly say I have no clue. Duncan, it was nice meeting you." Quickly excusing herself from the table, Mona rushed away from them.

"Is everyone afraid of your brother?" He sat down beside her.

"Well, they've seen how he reacted the last time a guy grabbed my ass. We'd just left CS and, to be honest, the guy had to go to the hospital."

"Why? I know for a fact you can protect yourself." He couldn't help grinning at the memory of her punching him. The thought of her doing it again was enough to make his cock twitch with interest inside his pants.

"Yeah, and he knows I can. But I think to him I'll always just be his baby sister, you know?"

"Not really." He shook his head. "And I can honestly say I've never regretted it. I was glad when my parents didn't have anymore kids. They said I was more than enough for them to handle by myself. They weren't sure they could handle another child, especially if I taught it all my tricks."

72

"That was so mean of them."

"Not really, they were absolutely right. I raised a lot of hell in my day. I was forever ignoring all the rules, and doing what I wanted. And they were also right when they thought I'd teach any siblings my tricks. Not all of them, mind you, but enough to make my mom's hair turn gray. Or should I say grayer? Her beautiful black hair was almost snow white by the time I finished puberty," he told her with a chuckle.

There was a lull in the conversation. Unable to stand the confusion, the not knowing any longer, he blurted out, "Did you change your mind?"

"About?"

He arched an eyebrow.

"Oh, that. N-No, I didn't. Why did you?"

She looked afraid; so young and vulnerable that even though he knew he should break things off between them, he couldn't. He couldn't reinforce that all men were complete pricks who were only interested in one thing.

He knew men who weren't like that. Like Bram. Bram was a man who deserved a woman like Melissa. He'd say and do all the right things and quickly help her forget about the horrors in her past. But the thought of Bram holding her in his arms pissed him off.

"No, Angel, I didn't change my mind. How could I when you look so beautiful?" Looking around, he motioned for the door. "Wanna get out of here?"

"Where would we go?"

"Anywhere you want to go."

"Even to a movie about knights?" A look of mischief was on her face.

With a groan, his head flopped forward until it hit the table. "Even a movie about knights," he told her grumpily.

Laughing, she was shaking her head when he looked up. Standing up, she took his hand and preceded him out of the club.

Outside, she stood on her tiptoes to give him a quick kiss on the cheek. "You are something else, do you know that?"

Motioning for him stay where he was, Melissa climbed into a taxi and leaned closer to the driver, whispering their destination in his ear.

She'd made certain he stayed far enough back that he couldn't hear what she told the driver over his radio.

When the driver nodded, she gestured for Duncan to climb in.

"That was just wrong. I said I'd go to the movies." He sulked, curious to know where they were going.

"Yes, but tonight I want you at my mercy. I don't want you to know where we're going until we get there."

Arching his eyebrow, he looked around. "And how are you going to accomplish that?"

Images of Melissa leaning, kissing him as her tongue thrust into his mouth filled his head. He wanted to pull her onto his lap, to bury his face in her neck, breathe her scent deeply.

"Hey," he said, taken by complete shock when she covered his eyes with her hands.

"It's a surprise."

Scooping her up, he pulled her onto his lap.

"What are you doing?"

"I'm just enjoying the ride, Angel." Laying his head against her shoulder, he felt like he was in heaven.

Chapter Six

The look on his face when she took him into the bowling alley was worth any embarrassment sitting on his lap had caused. Of course she'd wanted to pull him closer when he rested his head on her shoulder. She wanted to cradle him to her breast until he helped them both to forget about everything but the present.

"What are we doing here?"

"You said we could go anywhere I wanted," she teased.

"Yeah, but I thought you wanted to go to see some movie."

"Nah. Not tonight. Unless you're disappointed...I mean, if you had your heart set on seeing some knight movie—"

"Nope, not at all."

At the counter they ordered their shoes and moved to a lane.

"I didn't think you were a bowler."

"Well, I didn't say I was any good at it," she told him with a smile. "But it's fun and it's not Club Strigoi. And my brother is nowhere to be seen." She made a show of looking around.

"True. I was beginning to wonder if you were avoiding me, when you didn't come back to the club." He picked up his ball and rolled it down the lane, knocking over at least seven of the pins.

"I wanted to give you some space to decide if you were sure you still wanted to go through with the dating thing. I won't blame you if you've changed your mind. After all, not only do you have to deal with my screwed up past, but my brother's been suspected of doing more than just trying to intimidate guys around me. We get a mystery card with no signature every Christmas, I think it's from the hospital. But they don't want him to know how much they appreciate him sending so much business."

Duncan surprised her by laughing. "Oh Angel, your brother doesn't scare me. There are scarier guys in this world than him, and you're with one of them right now."

"Really? Then why aren't I afraid? Why do you always seem to want to avoid running into my brother while you're with me?"

"Because I'm not stupid. Mel, I know you love your brother and I don't want to hurt you because I had to hurt him." Rolling the ball down the aisle again, he got a spare. "And you never have anything to fear around me."

"I've already been lucky enough to have one knight in shining armor. What if I don't need another one?"

"Then I will sigh in relief. My armor was never shiny. It was always more of the tarnished variety."

Standing poised to take her turn, Melissa started laughing so hard that the ball slipped out of her hand and went almost directly into the gutter. Walking to the ball return to retrieve it, she shoved Duncan playfully.

"No fair. You made me laugh."

"Haven't you heard?" There was a twinkle in his eyes. "All's fair in love and bowling."

Giggling, she rolled her ball. "I'll have to remember that."

Glancing over her shoulder, she paused when she thought she saw someone watching them, but whoever it was stayed too far away for her to see who it was. Positive it was just one of her friends trying to protect her, she dismissed the man watching them.

ᕫᔓᕬ

The game was almost over. Duncan was rolling his last set. As he pulled his arm back to roll the ball, he felt a hand grab his ass. Releasing the ball a second too early, it went straight into the gutter of the lane—three aisles over from them.

Looking back, he laughed when Melissa tried to act innocent.

"I'm so sorry, I didn't distract you did I?"

"You are evil. But I'm still going to win." He kissed the tip of her nose, fighting the desire to pull her into his arms right then. Though his cock wasn't hard, it had remained at half-mast all night. And around Melissa, it wouldn't take much for it become fully erect again.

Grabbing a ball—any ball—he approached the lane for his last roll.

"You were the one that said 'All's fair in love and bowling'," she reminded him with a laugh.

"This is true. But I'm prepared now, nothing will distract me again," he bluffed.

"Okay."

Part of him was disappointed that she wouldn't try again. But he focused his mind on the game.

Once again, just as he was about to release the ball she made her move. No simple caress, this time she bit his waist.

The ball slipped from his fingers, dropping solidly on his foot, but even that didn't help the suddenly painful hard-on he now had.

"Oh gods, I am so sorry," she told him, her voice panicked.

Though he didn't need it, he let her "help" him over to the chairs. True his foot hurt like a bitch, but he'd gladly drop another bowling ball on it—in the same spot—if it meant she'd bite him again.

"I'm so sorry, Duncan. I just thought it would hit the gutter again." Kneeling in front of his chair she unlaced his shoe to pull his foot out and take a look at it.

"I'm fine, Angel," he told her hoarsely.

"You don't sound fine, mister. Maybe we should call an ambulance?" someone nearby asked.

"I don't need—"

"Do you think he got hurt that badly?" Melissa's eyes were wide with fear.

"What happened?" a woman asked as a crowd formed around them.

"He should go to the hospital. He's probably got broken bones," another added.

He wanted to smack them. He knew they were only trying to be helpful, but with each comment Melissa's eyes grew wider; her panic and guilt increasing.

"I'm fine," he said in a loud voice. Looking at her, he repeated more gently, "Really, I'm fine."

"That's impossible," said some know-it-all voice in the crowd. "No one could be fine after having a bowling ball fall on their foot."

"I am. I'm just really lucky I grabbed the wrong ball." To prove his point he gently pried Melissa's hands from around his ankle and stood up. Forcing back a wince, he smiled and took a few steps. "See, perfectly fine."

After a minute or two the crowd saw they weren't going to get any more of a show and dispersed.

"Are you really okay?" Clearly still concerned for him, she wouldn't let the matter drop.

"Angel, I'm fine. Remember, I heal really quickly."

She looked skeptical but eventually accepted his comment. But he could still feel her guilt. It was touching in a twisted sort of way. She'd hurt him, completely unintentionally, and she grieved for causing him pain. No one had ever cared if he was hurt before.

Paying for their game, he ignored her protests then led her out of the building.

"I am so sorry…"

On the empty street he pulled her into his arms. Kissing her gently, he silenced her apology.

"I know you are, Angel." Duncan reluctantly released her and they resumed their walk.

"Does it still hurt?"

He considered lying to her, but discarded the idea. "A little, yes."

"Then we shouldn't be walking." She pointed across the street then tugged on his hand.

Entering the playground, Melissa released his hand and ran over to the swings. His pain was forgotten when he saw her laughing as she sat down on a swing. He wondered what she was like as a child. He could easily picture her laughing and smiling all the time.

His thoughts turned from innocent thoughts and shifted to a much more carnal nature when he saw the way she pumped her legs and arched her back just so in order to push the swing higher.

Walking over to her, he leaned on one of the metal supports. "Tell me about your childhood."

Her smile vanished.

"I meant before your mom died," he added.

Nodding, she let the swing slow down. "She was a great woman. I mean, sure she didn't play with me all the time, but I never felt ignored. She'd take me to the playground and smile and laugh as I ran around. I remember this one time that she came to school and got me out of class.

"She told the teachers that I had an appointment she'd forgotten about. But as soon as we were out of the building she laughed and raced me to the car. When I asked where we were going she looked at me so seriously and said, 'Today is such a beautiful day. It would've been a crime for you to miss it.'

"We went to the grocery store and got some supplies, then went to the almost empty playground. She'd put a blanket in the trunk and we laid it on the grass. We sat there having a picnic while my friends were stuck in school.

After we finished she bought me ice cream and we ran all over the playground. We swung on the swings together, climbed the jungle gym. She even slid down the slides with me.

"And when kids started crowding us, she winked and told me it was time to go. She took me to a movie I wanted to see and even threw some popcorn on me."

To Duncan it seemed as though Melissa's face glowed as she spoke about her mom.

"Then when I should've been in bed, she took me to play miniature golf. We raced go-karts and splashed each other in the boats. When we finally did go home, she gave me a big hug and kissed my forehead. She looked at me and said 'I know I'm not always the most fun mom in the world. But I hope you know that I always love you. That I do treasure the time we do spend together, and I couldn't be more proud of the lady you are becoming.'

"I was only in elementary school, but I was becoming a 'lady'. None of my friends could understand my smile the next day at school, but I never told them of the day we'd spent together. It was our day, our secret, and she was the best mom in the world." Shaking her head, she wiped a tear from her eye. "Tell me about your childhood. Why did you become an assassin?"

"There's not much to tell. I was born a vampire. We lived in a mansion in England. My mom and dad never denied me anything. I'd like to say they were mean or they ignored me—that's what everyone expects, but it's not true. They loved me more than anything.

"As for why I became an assassin, I don't really know. It's not like I enjoyed torturing animals or anything. One night, when I was about forty or so, I saw this guy attacking a woman. I pulled him off her, but I hadn't fed yet. The smell of blood made me really hungry, but I wasn't going to drink from the woman that was hurt. Without really meaning to, I drained the guy dry, then grabbed his knife and slit his throat to hide my bite.

"Some of the queen's guards came to investigate and saw me wiping off his blade. They grabbed me for killing the man and trying to rape the woman.

She stopped them, told them I'd saved her life, thankfully leaving out the part where I'd drunk his blood.

"To make a long story short, she was one of Queen Anne's favorite courtiers, and a sorceress. Her Majesty had me trained as a member of her secret guard. I was taught how to hurt people without killing them, how to torture them to learn information, how to kill. I loved and respected Anne, serving her without fail.

"But then she was gone, and the politics changed, and suddenly I was told to kill the people that I'd previously been told to protect. When I refused, my parents were killed. I didn't know who was responsible at first and thought I'd been betrayed by those I'd protected.

"Loyalties were changed more often than clothes. I was told it didn't matter whom I was told to kill, just that I did my job. I decided if I was going to be an assassin, at least I was going to be my own boss. I was tired of working for petty royals with fickle whims. So, I left my home and England completely, coming over to America. Here it was easy enough to find out who was who.

"Starting with smaller jobs, I made a reputation for myself. The bosses didn't realize that I wasn't working for any of them exclusively. After a few years of killing for them, I left their 'employ'—as if I'd ever really worked for them in the first place. They'd have tried to kill me, but my reputation for playing with my victims had gotten around. No one would dare try to end my life. The rest is history."

"Wow. From average guy to guard to mobster to professional hit man to a bouncer. No one can say your life's been boring."

"That it certainly hasn't."

Melissa stood up and took his hand. Duncan allowed her to lead him over to a bench. When they sat down she snuggled close against him, resting her head on his shoulder.

Looking up at the stars, he wondered how he'd ever become so lucky.

"Duncan?"

Lowering his head, he planned on answering her question, but she didn't give him the chance. Her lips were on his. Desire flooded his body. Duncan pulled her closer, his tongue thrusting eagerly into her mouth as she sucked on it.

He trailed kisses down to her neck, his teeth scraping against her flesh, but he was careful not to taste her blood, never to break skin or scratch her.

Cupping her breast in his hand, he wanted to carry her over to a patch of grass and have sex with her beneath the stars. He wanted to give her another happy playground memory, but it wasn't the time.

Forcing himself to slow down, to pull back slightly and cool off, he resumed their conversation.

"You know I still won that game, right?"

"Why are you acting like this?" she asked without looking at him. "One minute you're all over me and the next you're talking like we didn't—like nothing happened. Didn't you feel…"

"Angel, I promised we would go slow." Gently grasping her hand, he put it on his jean-covered erection. "Yes, I felt it, but I won't let myself get so carried away that I say 'fuck it'. You deserve better than to be tossed down on the grass and fucked."

Nodding her understanding, she elbowed him gently. "Now that I know the rules of bowling with you, I'll be more prepared the next time we play."

"Uh-oh," he teased. "Prepared how?"

"Nothing big. I'll just make sure I've thought up all kinds of ways to distract you."

"Note to self, I'm gonna need steel-toe bowling shoes."

Melissa laughed and leaned against his chest.

"So when do you want to go again? Cause I can be free tomorrow night…" Duncan told her with a smile.

Still laughing she shoved him playfully. In the darkness, Duncan wondered yet again what he could have done to deserve a treasure like her.

They sat there talking and occasionally making out for most of the night. As dawn slowly crept closer, Duncan hailed a taxi and took her home. He took her in his arms and kissed her good night as the taxi driver waited.

"Did you want to come in…" she asked shyly.

"More than you know. And that's why I'm gonna go home."

Melissa sighed. "Then I guess I'll see you later."

After one more too quick kiss, she entered the house, and he returned to the taxi. Giving the driver the address, Duncan leaned back and thought about Melissa.

He could already tell he was growing attached to her. He didn't want to hurt her, and the thought of her with another man made his fangs lengthen.

It was wrong of him to continue seeing her, but he wasn't strong enough to give her up. He wanted her to know just how valuable she was, and determined to treat her like the most priceless of treasures for as long as they were together.

Being realistic, he wouldn't allow himself to think they had a future together, that she'd want to be with him for eternity. But he knew he'd treasure her for as long as she allowed him to.

Walking through the club, Duncan went upstairs, sighing. As hard as his cock was after making out with Melissa half the night, he knew he'd have to do something before he went to sleep.

Entering the small windowless room he'd insisted on taking for his own, Duncan stripped and entered the bathroom. With warm water flowing all around him, he closed his eyes, conjuring her image. Remembering how she felt pressed against him, he groaned.

Closing his hand around his cock, he used every ounce of his imagination to change it into Mel's hand. To melt away the familiar calluses until all he felt was her smooth, delicate, sinfully soft palm caressing his flesh.

Her hand moved slowly up and down his length, pausing to trace the lines and curve of its head. He could just imagine her short fingernail tracing circles around the tip of his cock, each circle growing smaller and smaller until she reached the center and the precome that had leaked out just for her.

Being the inquisitive woman that she was, he knew she would lean over slightly for a closer look. Would she lean over and taste the clear liquid waiting there for her? Would she slide her finger over top of it and rub it into his cock? Anticipation driving him crazy, he relished the trip as he awaited her next move.

Surprising him, Melissa looked up into his face as she slowly dragged the tip of her tongue across the top, scooping it up and tasting him. Her hand moved to the base of his erection before she released him. Using only one finger she lightly scraped her nail over his balls, swirling around them slowly.

Despite the fact that he felt ready to explode at her simple ministrations, he fought to maintain control. He wanted to enjoy her touch for as long as he could. Stopping her hand with his own for just a moment while he struggled with his body's desire to come, he released her when the urge had weakened slightly.

A twinkle in her eye, Melissa glanced at him and began to move her hand slowly. The smile curving her lips told him that she knew what effect she was having on his body, and that she enjoyed it. A groan escaped him when she squeezed him just-so right beneath the head of his cock.

Her pace increased little by little. Growing bolder, she continued stroking him with one hand as the other joined in. Her previously free hand cupped his balls first, her short nails lightly scratching against his flesh until he was growling with pleasure. Beneath her touch, his balls grew tighter, and he knew that this time he would not be able to stop the orgasm.

Taking her hand off his balls, she moved it to the head of his cock, squeezing it gently in rhythm to her strokes. Duncan's head fell back and he thought he was in heaven as his eyes started to roll back in his head.

Beneath the shower's spray, his hand sped up until his orgasm ripped through his body and come was being washed down the drain.

He dried himself off and returned to the bedroom. Scooping up the phone before he lay down, Duncan called an old friend of his. When the voicemail picked up, he left a message.

"Jake, it's Duncan. I was wondering if you'd be willing to come by the club sometime. I've been thinking about getting something pierced and was wondering if you'd be up for it. Give me a call back sometime. Catch you later."

Hanging up the phone, Duncan placed it on the small table beside his bed and drifted off to sleep.

CREO

Inside the deserted warehouse he was calling his temporary home, Travis fumed. That worthless slut Diane hadn't been able to find out anything about this mystery man. He'd wanted to rush over to them as they sat in that playground and drive a stake into the bastard's heart when he saw the way he was touching Melissa. She was his property damn it, and no other man should be groping her like that!

At least now he was sure the man wasn't human. No human could take a bowling ball to the foot like that and simply walk out of there as though nothing had happened. No, any normal man would have gone straight to the hospital.

Looking around, he tried to find something that he could vent his rage on, but the place was nearly empty. His gaze landed on the bed. It was his one and only luxury item. It had a wrought iron frame. When he saw it, he'd known he had to have it. He could imagine his step-bitch tied to it. The metal would ensure that she couldn't break her way free. And once he had her strapped to the bed, right where he wanted her, that's when the payback would begin, when the fun would start.

Shifting his focus to a thick beam that disappeared high into the ceiling, Travis could see that brown-haired bastard that stole Melissa from him. He could see him wrapped in silver chains, struggling against the burning, forced to watch as Travis found pleasure in discovering all the tricks that vampire and all his friends had taught her. Then, when he was screaming in helpless rage, Travis would get his revenge. He'd become the cat, toying with his prey.

He'd enjoy scorching the unholy creature with the small silver crucifixes that he'd bought.

A roll of duct tape lay near the beam on a small wooden table. He had big plans for that, after all, it was such a versatile tool. The monster would have his mouth sealed shut by it, after Travis had slipped one of the crosses into his mouth. He wouldn't get to see the foaming he was sure would be present, but he could imagine how badly the creature would writhe in pain, his muffled screams almost a symphony to his ears.

And for Melissa, well, he had much more creative ideas about what he'd do with her. He'd make her beg him to forgive her. He'd make her wish she'd just been a good girl all those years ago instead of running away and humiliating him.

When she ran off, he'd been a laughing stock. But now…now all that was going to change, and he was going to relish his revenge.

Pulling his dick out, he started to jerk off as he closed his eyes and remembered the look of fear she used to get in her eyes when he raised his hand. After a few smacks, the simple gesture was enough to ensure she did exactly as she was told.

He'd waited patiently for her bitch mother to die so he could have her all to himself. And now all that waiting would pay off.

Stopping his movements, he tucked himself back into his jeans. The urge to come was almost overwhelming, but he would wait. At least until after he called Diane. The slut would meet him someplace, and since she seemed so incompetent in earning her money by being his spy, he'd make certain she earned it another way.

He would make sure she wore the brown wig too. If he squinted just right, he was almost able to fool himself into thinking it was Melissa.

And after he'd come by ramming his dick down her throat until he was satisfied, he'd make sure she got a taste of what would happen if she continued to fail to get the information he wanted.

Chapter Seven

"Don't worry, Gareth's at La's." Melissa teased Duncan as he entered her house. Taking his hand, she led him into the living room and sat down on the couch. "Is it horrible for me to admit I feel like I'm back in high school?" she asked nervously.

"Why?"

"Well, going bowling, making out in the playground, you coming over to watch a movie…it's just how I imagined dating would be in high school."

Duncan put his arm around her. "Is that so bad?"

"No. But I'm not in high school. I'm a grown woman, and I feel like I have to sneak around behind my brother's back."

"We don't have to sneak around. I'm not afraid of your brother, Angel."

"But I don't want either of you to get hurt." She was silent for a few minutes then pushed off the couch. "So, what movie do you want to watch?"

"I get a choice?" He gasped, playing along with her earlier teasing manner.

"Not if you keep talking like that." Kneeling in front of the entertainment center, Melissa looked through their collection of movies. Smiling, she grabbed a movie she'd seen a hundred times before. "What about this?" She held it up.

"That's fine."

"Cool. I love this movie." Putting it into the DVD player she went around the room, cutting off the lights. A thought struck her, and she went to the fridge to grab a couple bottles of water, and finally settled down beside Duncan.

After pressing play, she snuggled against his side. He put his arm around her again and they began watching the movie.

As always, Melissa became engrossed in the movie. It sucked her in. No matter how strange that family might be, they clearly loved all of their children, valued them—valued family—as a treasure.

Smiling, she moved closer to Duncan as the husband and wife danced. His arm went around her shoulders. Ignoring the timid voice inside her that shouted *"Stop, watch the movie"*, she sat a little straighter, pressing a kiss to his neck.

He made a slight sound in his throat but never stopped her. Shifting her position on the couch, she knelt beside him, her mouth working a path up his neck to his ear. Sucking his earlobe into her mouth, she half gasped, half giggled when Duncan growled and pulled her onto his lap, sitting her across it.

"What are you doing," he asked huskily.

"I don't know. Whatever I want?"

"That's a good enough answer for me." His voice was rough as she continued her assault.

"You've been able to tease me, to play with me, but I haven't had a chance to see what gets you all hot and bothered. Let me know if you want me to stop." She breathed over his skin, a second before she nibbled on his neck.

With every sound that he made, Melissa's desire increased. All the other guys she'd ever gone out with—not that it was a large number—had always acted as though she completely lacked any sex appeal. Duncan, however, made certain she knew how much he wanted her. Without ever pressuring her for sex.

Feeling his hard cock pressing against her leg, she decided to move. Climbing off his lap, she immediately sank back down on top of him, but straddling him this time.

For a few seconds she simply sat there, perfectly still, torn between the urge to jump off him and the urge to arch against him in an attempt to get closer. He was pressed intimately against her and Melissa closed her eyes to try to control her fear.

"It's alright, Angel." Duncan rubbed her back. His body moved beneath her, as though he were going to move her from him.

"Don't." Opening her eyes, she looked into his. "It's not like you haven't been between my legs before," she teased. "I just...I just need a minute."

"I don't want you to do something because you think I want you to."

"And if I want to do it because of me?"

He gently kissed her lips. "Then I'll give you all the time in the world."

Laying her head on his shoulder, she reminded herself that he wasn't going to hurt her. He'd had the perfect opportunity, not once but twice now.

Closing her eyes again, Melissa concentrated on how his hands felt on her back. Snuggling closer, she kissed his neck again, nibbling occasionally as she worked her way up to his mouth.

Straddling his waist, she shifted closer to him seconds before she took his face in her hands and kissed him. The hands on her waist gripped her a little harder, but she didn't care. Duncan's tongue entered her mouth and she gave up on thinking completely. She gave herself permission to simply feel. Moaning into his mouth, she arched her hips against him, wanting to feel him closer still.

The kiss ended, leaving her breathless. Removing his hands from her waist, she wanted to feel his hands on her bare skin. But he misinterpreted the action.

"I'm sorry, Angel. I didn't mean to get so rough with you. Maybe we should sto—"

Swooping on his lips, she refused to let him finish that sentence. As she kissed him, her hands yanked the edge of her shirt from the waist of her jeans. Releasing his mouth, she slid back far enough to lift her shirt over her head.

"Are you sure you know—"

Again she cut him off, this time placing her finger against his mouth.

"I'm not really thinking right now. But in a good way," she added quickly. "I just want to feel you pressed against me, not my shirt."

He nodded, his hands moving to her back, stroking her flesh.

"Do you know how incredibly beautiful you are?" he asked her, kissing her neck, then her shoulder.

"Tell me?"

He chuckled against her skin, his mouth never ceasing the magick he wove over her. When he bit down on her shoulder she gasped. She'd allowed her brother to drink from her occasionally—though always on her wrist. Duncan's action was similar, but she knew he wasn't drinking from her. She knew he wouldn't drink from her without permission. The sensations his slight bite caused coursed down her body and pooled in her pussy, until she wanted to arch against him again.

Giving in to the urge, she arched her back as his mouth continued to progress down her body until it rested on the swell of her breast. She felt him growling against her, but he never tried to remove her bra. His lips slid over the lacy material, the feeling incredibly erotic, especially when he gently nipped her erect nipple.

A sound escaped her throat, and straightening, Melissa ripped at his shirt in an attempt to remove the obstacle. She wanted to feel his bare chest against her, wanted to run her fingers over his unique tattoo, to see how it would taste beneath her tongue.

Duncan complied, quickly yanking his shirt off when Melissa tugged on it. He wanted so badly to rip the rest of their clothes off and bury himself inside of her.

Groaning as her covered pussy ground against him again, he wondered how much temptation, how much enticement a man could take before he went insane.

Curious, he allowed her to push him against the back of the couch. Her tongue traced the outline of his tattoo and he thought he would come in his pants. She was so gentle, as though she were scared to hurt him. As she licked his chest, her hips continued to grind into him.

His fingers arched, scratching down her back then grasping her hips. Gods, he did not want her to stop. Her tongue swirled over his nipple before she bit down on him, in perfect imitation of his earlier fondling.

Guiding her hips, he thrust upwards. Ignoring the fact that they both still had their jeans on, he moved exactly as he would if he were able to bury himself inside of her.

After a few strokes like that, of pulling her hard down onto him and her grinding into his erection, her head fell backwards. Her breathing sounded labored and her heart beat irregularly. Not one to pass up such a tempting treat, he leaned forward, never stopping his pseudo-thrusting and licked and suckled the swells of her breasts.

Careful to only allow his teeth to graze her, but never actually pierce her skin, he sucked her flesh into his mouth, working in time to the movement of his hips.

His teeth ached to be buried in her until it was an almost physical pain, much the way his cock throbbed, pressing against his jeans in an attempt to get to the pussy it knew was so close.

Speeding up his movements, he pressed up, grinding her harder into him until he heard her cry out, her body trembling under his hands.

His own body screamed at him, berating him for stopping when he was so close to his own release. But Duncan refused to come in his pants like some teenaged boy.

Biting down on his lip, he tasted the fresh blood just before he continued to suckle Melissa's breast, fooling his body into thinking it would be at least slightly appeased.

Releasing her, he looked up at her passion-glazed eyes.

"Sorry about that."

"Huh?" A look of shock came over her face. "Duncan, if you apologize for that so help me I will—"

Pulling her closer to him roughly, he followed her earlier example and stopped the threat before she could finish it.

Releasing her, he chuckled. "Oh Angel, I'm never sorry for that. I was actually apologizing for that." His fingers circled then caressed the mark he'd left on her breast.

"Oh. Well…in that case, I guess it's a good thing I don't wear low-cut shirts."

"Yes, it is. I'm not sure if I could handle seeing you in such a revealing top."

"I don't think I'd look *that* bad in one," she sulked.

Another chuckle escaped. "Angel, this is what you do to me." He placed her hand between their bodies and on his still swollen cock. "Imagine how much worse it would be if you did wear that kind of clothing. Besides, I know for a fact Bram would get really pissed at me if I tried to kill anyone inside his club."

"Why would you…"

Instead of answering the question, he kissed her tenderly. He wasn't ready to admit out loud that he thought he was falling in love with her. Hell, he wasn't even ready to admit it to himself.

The television and their movie completely forgotten, Duncan and Melissa kissed.

C33O

Groaning in the control room, Duncan wished someone—anyone— would go into the backroom to fuck. The past few nights he'd had some of the most incredible make-out sessions of his life, but he was feeling the strain.

Watching the monitor in the backroom closely, it seemed as though his wish was about to be granted. A couple entered the room, the man sure, the woman a little timid.

Going to the couch, the man put his arm around her shoulders then kissed her neck. His free hand moved to grasp her breast, and she shrugged him off. Looking at him, the woman said something, shaking her head.

Warning bells went off inside of Duncan's head when the guy ignored her and resumed groping her. Duncan's teeth lengthened and his hands curled into fists as he forced himself to remain and watch. He'd seen a semi-reluctant partner become all too willing too many times in the past to rush in before he was sure the situation warranted it.

Once again, he saw the woman on the screen push the man away. This time she attempted to stand up, but the man jerked her back down onto the green cushions. He couldn't hear what they were saying—damn Bram and his belief that there should be some privacy in that room—but from the look on the man's face, Duncan would guess he was yelling.

The woman looked scared, cringing back as far as she could from him, which wasn't far given his grip on her arm.

Not caring to see what happened next, Duncan practically flew down the stairs and out the door leading to the club. Looking at the first bouncer he saw, he gruffly ordered, "You. Up there. Now."

The man didn't argue, or waste any time. Practically running, he disappeared through the door Duncan just exited.

His position covered, Duncan sped through the club, shoving people out of his way as he took the quickest route to the backroom. At the door he forced himself to take a deep breath and tried to turn the knob.

It was no use. The fucker had locked the door. Reaching into his pocket he pulled out the only key he always carried with him and unlocked the door. After another—quick—deep breath to control his temper, he opened the door, trying to act as casual as possible.

Glancing at the clock first, he noticed less than two minutes had passed since he left the control room. Looking over at the couch, he saw the girl holding her cheek, protecting her eye, cringing on a corner of the couch as the man fumbled with his pants.

"Hey, what's going on?" Duncan asked innocently.

"None of your business, asshole," the man answered without looking back.

"Are you okay?" Duncan asked the woman. Her eyes were wide, but she didn't answer him. "If you don't want to be back here with him, you don't have to stay. You can leave whenever you want."

She looked at him hopefully, and tried to inch her way off the couch.

"If you move, you'll wish you hadn't," the man spit out.

"You can leave if you want to," Duncan told her again, approaching them.

"I told you before, mind your own business." The man whirled around, a knife in his hand. "Before I make you regret sticking your nose in where it don't belong."

Before Duncan even realized what he was doing, the knife was on the floor, the man's arm broken, and his nose bleeding. Grabbing the man by the collar, he looked back at the woman.

"I'll be right back." Shoving the man out the door, he threw him at the first bouncer he saw, thankfully the man was also vampire. "Take this trash out." He turned to reenter the room. "Oh, and he might need to go to the hospital."

Not waiting to hear what, if anything, the other bouncer had to say, Duncan returned to the woman, still sitting on the couch.

Sitting down beside her, he noticed she was crying.

"It's okay, that dick is being thrown out now."

"I'm so stupid," she cried. "I should've known."

Releasing a breath, he asked, "Do you want to talk about it?"

She shook her head no, and he wanted to sag against the couch with relief. He hated being the one left to comfort a near victim. He sucked at it.

"It's just, that guy's my ex, and he swore things had changed. He swore he had changed, that he was in anger management classes. He swore it would be different..." Her voice broke as she cried harder. "I should have known it was too good to be true. I should've known he'd never change. If you hadn't come in here..."

"But I did. Do you want to press charges on him? For hitting you?"

The woman looked up, her eye already swelling shut.

"Y-yes. But I can't...I..."

"Come on, I know someone that'll take you down there, help you with all the paper work." Moving to the lockers, he opened one and reached on the top shelf, grabbing a card. Closing the door, he handed her the business card. "This has the club's number and address, and my name on it, in case you need to contact me."

Guiding her to the door gently, he ushered her to one of the human bouncers. "Tim, take this pretty lady to the police station. She wants to press charges for assault. And help her fill out a restraining order too." Looking at the woman, he smiled. "Tim's a great guy, he'll make sure you don't get hurt."

"Where should I tell them to pick up the guy?" Tim asked, already wrapping a protective arm around the woman.

"Hospital. Bastard pulled a knife on me. No major injuries, he should be out in a few hours."

Tim nodded and, gently guiding her thanks to the arm he had around her, escorted her out of the club.

Turning around, he saw Melissa watching him. Tonight he didn't care if Gareth walked up on them or if he started shit. He strode over to her table. He needed to calm down before he put another guy in the hospital that night.

Instead of sitting down, he pulled her out of her seat, and onto the dance floor. Moving until they were in the middle of the floor, he held her in his arms as they danced together. Her presence soothed the nerves left raw by dealing with a jerk.

Of all the things he hated the most, breaking up a near rape in the backroom was his least favorite. Men who tried to take by force what a woman would—should—give willingly infuriated him. He shuddered, his thoughts returning to what the woman had said. If he'd been even a minute later, he wouldn't have been in time.

And then Bram would have been pissed, because they'd have needed to call an ambulance. Or a coroner.

"Rough night?" Melissa stepped closer to him in the dance.

"Yes."

When she moved, Duncan wanted to fall to his knees from gratitude. Instead of moving away from him, or asking him twenty questions about what happened, she pulled him to her. Turning her back on him, she danced with him, moving against him intimately. Melissa circled around him until he could feel her breasts pressed against his back.

Without knowing what she was doing, she managed to cage the animal roaring inside him to go finish his job, to make sure that bastard could never try to hurt another woman.

Without trying, Melissa was somehow able to soothe the savage beast within him.

Chapter Eight

Watching the monitors in front of him, Duncan wished he were anywhere else. He'd been in a relationship with Melissa for two weeks and he'd kept a hard-on almost the entire time. He wished Bram would come relieve him for a little while so he could go take yet another cold shower, maybe try to jerk off again. But he knew that wasn't likely to happen. Not since that woman, Dani, had begun to come to the club every night.

Glancing over the monitors, he found the one he was looking for, the one that showed Bram and Dani talking. He wondered if both really were that clueless to the attraction between them. Searching the monitors, he smiled when he saw Melissa sitting at a table, alone. Shaking his head, he stood up. Leaving the control room he tapped one of the other bouncers to go upstairs for a while. The man looked at him skeptically.

"I'm not going to have to clean the room am I?"

"No," he growled. The bouncer nodded and slipped silently through the door. Thankfully it didn't appear as though his exit had been noticed by many patrons.

The post covered, Duncan moved through the crowd, glaring at any woman who tried to brush against him until he reached his destination.

"Hey, beautiful," he said, placing a kiss against Melissa's neck. He knew he took her by surprise when her elbow connected with his nose.

"I'm so sorry. You have to stop doing that," she scolded him as she pressed a piece of ice from her water to his nose.

He couldn't help laughing at the situation. Her reactions were always so varied. "I think I'm beginning to like it," Duncan teased, earning him a shove on the arm. "You wanna get out of here for a while?" Wrapping his arms around her, he awaited her answer.

"And where did you want to go?"

"Someplace quiet, without an audience. Or at least one without a guy who will happily try to rip the head off my body."

"Okay."

Moments later, they were on the street. "How have you been sleeping?"

"Some days better than others." She shrugged. "I still wake up from nightmares now and then, but at least it's not every day anymore."

"I'm glad. So, what's helping the nightmares?"

"You know good and well what's helping." Melissa bumped into him.

"Yeah, but it's nice to have my ego stroked now and then." He clasped her hand in his and brought it to his lips.

"Duncan?" She moaned his name. He loved her reaction to him. It was always so honest, so real and free.

"Yes, Angel?" He nibbled on her knuckle.

"Are you a sorcerer?"

"I've drank a few in my time," he teased. "No, Angel, I'm not."

"You make me feel... No other guy has ever..." She shook her head. "If you're not a sorcerer, then how can you be so magical? One kiss from you and I feel like everything melts away. I don't have a past, no one else exists, nothing else matters."

He looked at her. She was different from that first time he'd held her through the night. She was less guarded around him.

"I feel the same way," he told her honestly.

"Then why won't you—? Why haven't we—?"

"Oh, Angel, I just want you to be sure."

"I'm sure. I'm completely sure. If I take one more cold shower, I'm going to move to Alaska, or maybe Antarctica."

He chuckled.

"I'm not joking, Duncan."

He couldn't banish the smile from his lips. Holding her hand, he felt her begin to pull him in a direction. He didn't stop the chuckle when she hailed a taxi and gave the driver her address before climbing inside.

Sitting beside her, he pulled her close.

"I'm not joking, Duncan," she told him again. "I want—"

He placed a finger against her lips. "I know, Mel, I know."

CR80

A dark figure was on the street a half a block away from her house when the taxi finally dropped them off. But since it wasn't very late, she decided to ignore it. Besides, she hoped to be doing something more special with her night than worry about some stranger lurking in the shadows. Especially since he was probably just taking a walk.

Melissa unlocked the front door, her hands shaking slightly. She hoped Duncan wasn't watching her too closely. She was excited and scared, terrified and anxious. What if she couldn't please him? What if he changed his mind and wanted to be with someone else as soon as they had—

She shook her head to dislodge the thoughts. No. She was ready. More ready than she'd ever been before.

Opening the door she entered the house, knowing Duncan would follow her. She headed for the kitchen to get some water for her suddenly dry mouth.

"Nervous?" he asked in that way of his. The one that said it was all right to be feeling whatever she was feeling, the one that told her he accepted her as she was, with no pressure for anything.

She shrugged, but he would not be put off. "Melissa…"

"A little," she admitted. "But that doesn't mean I don't want to do it."

"It's a big step."

Melissa smiled and handed him the bottle, watching him drink from it. "I'm ready," she told him when he finished drinking. Taking his hand in hers she headed for the basement room. Over the last few weeks she'd grown to think of it as their room.

Inside the room, she stared at the bed, suddenly more nervous than she'd ever been before. What did they do now? Should she just start taking all of her clothes off? Should she wait for him to make a move? Sit on the bed and try to look seductive? Stand in the middle of the room and look like an idiot?

"Relax," Duncan told her, placing a kiss on her neck. "There's no rush." He gently pulled her to the bed. Sitting down, he tugged her down onto his lap. Her arms circled his neck automatically.

"I just feel so stup—"

"Shhh." His finger lay against her lips. "I don't ever want to hear you say that about yourself. Mel, I'm…well, I'm old and I've never met a woman that was braver or smarter than you are."

"I'm not brave." She shook her head vigorously, denying his praise. "I'm just a scared, stup—silly girl. I mean, there's nothing to be scared of right? Everyone does it. Aren't I a little old to be acting like some kind of cowering virgin? It's not like I don't know what happens. I watch TV. I've watched cable. You can't get more descriptive than some of those shows without actually being considered porn. I've read books…" she admitted, her face warming.

"See, that's just it. Those are actors, or fictional characters. It's one thing to see it happen on TV or read about it. And yes, there is a lot to be afraid of, it's a big step. What if you get pregnant? What if the guy's a dog and he just walks away when you're done, then never wants to talk to you again? What if he's a vampire and wants to drink from you? What if he's got something, a disease? What if you think you're ready but you're not?"

Melissa looked at him, her eyes practically bulging out of her face. He'd touched on a few of the things she was terrified of. Letting her brother take a quick nip was one thing, but did she really want Duncan to have an all access pass into her brain? "Are you trying to comfort me? Cause you know, not helping."

He chuckled, and pulled her close. "The point is that it's natural to be scared."

"Are you...?"

"Scared? No." He shook his head.

"No. Are you just gonna walk away and never gonna want to see me again?"

He forced her to look into his eyes. "No. I won't say I'm not that kind of man, cause I am. I've done it in the past." He shrugged. "But Mel, those women all knew, before anything happened, that I wouldn't be staying."

She nodded, understanding what he meant. "Are you gonna want to drink from me?"

"I won't if you say no."

"What if I don't like it? What if I'm no good?" The questions flew out of her mouth. Burying her head against Duncan's shoulder, she was too embarrassed to look him in the eye.

"Well, if you don't like it, then I did something wrong." He chuckled. His hands slid up and down her back, slightly massaging and helping her to relax. "As for no good, well, Angel, I doubt that."

"How can you be so sure?"

"Angel, I haven't been this worked up in at least a hundred years, and we haven't even gotten to the really good stuff."

"But, it could just be because you're horny. Maybe it doesn't have anything to do with me. Maybe it's just—"

He pressed a kiss to her lips, effectively silencing her. All questions and fears were forgotten as Melissa clung to him, kissing him back as she lost herself in the sensations that blazed through her body. Lifting her arms with his own when the kiss ended, they traveled back down her body to pull her shirt off.

Melissa pulled away from him, standing up. Keeping her eyes locked on his she unhooked her bra and dropped it to the floor. Taking a deep breath, Melissa prepared herself for what came next. Her hands went to her jeans and she unbuttoned them then slowly lowered the zipper. Before she could pull them down her hips, Duncan stopped her by pulling her back to his lap. This time she was straddling him. Tilting her head slightly she pressed close to him, kissing him hungrily.

She felt his hands gliding up and down her back, leaving delicious tingles everywhere he touched. Kissing her way down to his neck, she slid her tongue over his flesh, up to his ear. Sucking the lobe into her mouth, she bit down lightly on it, enjoying the way his fingers dug into her skin slightly.

His mouth lowered to her shoulder and his elongated fangs grazed against her, erotically. Her eyes closed, allowing her to concentrate on his blissful touch. Beneath her, Duncan shifted, leaning her back against the bed. His hand moved over her stomach, cupping the weight of her breast as he kissed her.

Duncan slid down her body and her eyes closed as he took her nipple into her mouth, teasing her with his fangs. His silky hair brushed against her as he continued to move down her stomach. When he stopped, Melissa opened her eyes to look down at him. His hands were poised on her jeans, a question in his eyes as he watched her. Nodding, she lifted her hips off the bed. He slowly pulled them down, kissing and nibbling a path over her leg as he removed the obstacle.

Melissa closed her eyes again, conjuring his image beneath her lids as her heartbeat began to increase. *He won't hurt me,* she told herself over and over again, willing herself to calm down.

"Angel?"

"I'm fine," she reassured him, praying that she was telling him the truth. *He's not Travis. He doesn't want to hurt me. I want this.* But try as she might, she was afraid. It was the first time she'd ever been underneath a man without her jeans protecting her.

As though he could read her mind, Duncan returned to her. Lying beside her, with his jean clad leg resting on only one of hers, he kissed her gently. When she tried to deepen the kiss he pulled back slightly. Teasing her with small, light kisses, he massaged her breast. Tangling her hands in his hair, she jerked him to her, sucking his lower lip into her mouth. But he would not be rushed. He kissed her leisurely, making her forget everything but him.

She felt his hand moving down her body. It felt so nice; his touch was whisper soft and enticing. He caressed her through her underwear, drawing a moan from her.

"Just tell me if you want me to stop," he whispered into her ear before suckling on her earlobe. His nimble fingers traced the cleft of her pussy lips, each pass causing the ache inside of her body to grow.

"Duncan," she moaned. Her voice sounded full of need, even to her. When he looked up at her, she lifted her hips once again.

He stared into her eyes for a moment, but didn't question her. Nibbling on the opposite leg, he pulled her underwear off, letting them join her jeans—wherever they were.

She watched him as he knelt between her legs, looking down at her body. She wanted to ask what was wrong, if he was disappointed in what he saw, but was terrified of breaking whatever spell he had woven around her.

"You're so beautiful, Angel."

Melissa smiled shyly. When he lowered himself to feast on her breasts, she closed her eyes, arching into him. It felt so nice to finally feel him pressed against her, with no clothes dampening the sensations. Her fingers began to toy with his hair, her nails grazing against his flesh and over his scalp as the need deep within her built.

She chuckled slightly when his hair tickled her side as his tongue traced a path down her stomach.

Her hips arched against his chest, but still he continued to tease her. He continued to slowly move down her body. She bit down on her lower lip when he placed her leg over his shoulder.

She could feel his breath, warm against her flesh. Arching her hips slightly, she felt a tender kiss placed on her pussy. Her eyes flew open and she struggled to sit up.

Without moving from his spot between her legs, Duncan asked, "Would you like me to stop?"

She shook her head. As his tongue parted her lips, grazing against her clit, her eyes closed and she fell back against the bed. *Oh dear gods,* she moaned inside her head. His mouth moved against her, his tongue dipping into her pussy. Her hands twisted in the comforter, balling handfuls of the material in her fist as she panted from his attention.

His tongue slid up between her lips again. Melissa's whimper turned quickly into a moan as a finger slowly filled her. He circled her clit, his mouth occasionally sucking it into his mouth as his finger moved in and out of her body.

"Gods," she cried out, her hips arching off the bed, wanting to feel more of him inside of her. There was a brief twinge of pain followed by a feeling of being filled more completely. Duncan increased the pace of his fingers as he sucked her clit into his mouth again. She wanted to cry out, to scream for him to keep going, but her throat felt too dry. The only sound she seemed able to make was a needy whimper as she silently begged him to keep going.

Her muscles began to tense in a familiar fashion. Her head moved back and forth on the bed as the sensations became so much more powerful than they were with her clothes on. Her back arched, then her hips, in an attempt to get closer to him. When she felt his mouth pull away from her, she quickly released the material bunched in her hands and grabbed handfuls of his hair, pressing him closer to her body. His chuckle vibrated through her, but she didn't care, she was so close.

His fingers matched the frantic pace her hips set. As an orgasm unlike any she had felt before ripped through her body she was distantly aware of his fingers withdrawing from her. Her thighs clenched together, pressing tightly against his head. His tongue moved over her as he growled next to her flesh.

Her muscles trembling, Melissa slowly released his head, too tired and relaxed to move anymore than she had to.

Duncan nibbled on her shoulder before pressing a kiss to her lips. She could smell herself, taste herself on him, but it didn't matter. The only thoughts she seemed able to form inside her head were "wow" and "My gods."

He gathered Melissa in his arms and after a second of pressing her against his chest, he lowered her to the crisp, cool sheets. She wanted to protest, she wanted to feel his arms around her again. She wanted him to hold her. After what felt like an eternity, he was laying behind her.

"Are you okay?" he asked.

"Mm-hmm."

"Tired?"

"Yes," she told him, her voice slightly hoarse.

He placed a tender kiss on her neck and she felt him lay back.

"Duncan, what do you get out of that? I mean, it felt wonderful—gods did it feel wonderful—but what does it do for you?"

"It brings me pleasure. Feeling you trembling like that, knowing that I've satisfied you makes me feel satisfied as well. It's something I enjoy. It's something I hope you won't mind me doing again sometime soon."

A smile curved her lips and seeped into her voice. "Anytime. Well, as long as you give me a chance to recover first."

His body shook with laughter.

"That wasn't sex, Duncan," she pointed out.

"I know."

"Don't you want to have sex with me?"

He was silent a moment. "Angel, I don't want to hurt you. You're so tight." She felt him move behind her. He pressed a kiss to her shoulder. "It's probably going to hurt the first time. You were so tight around my fingers, Angel. There are things I can do, to help. I just want to make sure that when

105

Sandy Lynn

the time comes, you don't have to be in anymore pain than absolutely necessary."

Melissa nodded her understanding. She could remember hearing plenty of girls in the locker room talking about how it hurt the first time they'd let their boyfriends fuck them. Even in her books, it almost always said there was a brief amount of pain the first time.

Her lids growing heavy, she tried to fight off a yawn. "Duncan?" she asked sleepily.

"Yes?"

"Why do you keep saying you're no good at this shit?"

"What do you mean?"

Turning so she faced him, she looked into his eyes. "From that first time we kissed you told me you suck at the comforting shit. But you don't. I don't think I've ever been more comfortable, felt safer with any man—other than my brother."

"Then you would definitely be the only woman I've ever met that finds me comforting," he teased.

"Duncan…"

"You should get some rest, Angel."

She wanted to protest, but didn't. But she would say what she felt first, before sleep claimed her. Closing her eyes, Melissa let the words escape seconds before she fell asleep.

"I love you."

Chapter Nine

Duncan gave a slight growl in his throat as he stretched on the bed. He wasn't ready to wake up. He wanted to stay in his dream. It was so real he could practically feel Melissa caressing him. He smiled as he remembered taking the time to remove his jeans before he fell asleep.

At first her movements were timid as she stroked him through his boxers, but after a few strokes, she reached into them and her finger traced him.

He thought he was going to die when she pulled him through the opening, her hand wrapping around him for a few brief strokes before her finger began to trace the head of his cock. He hissed when he felt her loose hair trailing over his thighs before her warm breath blew over him.

Duncan tried to shift slightly in the bed, his eyes flying open when he felt palms against his thighs, restraining him only seconds before a tongue began to slide over him.

Lifting himself to his elbows, Duncan couldn't believe his eyes when he saw Melissa kneeling naked between his legs. Her full concentration was on the hard cock in front of her.

"It feels so hard," she said, her fingers going back to tracing him. He wasn't sure if she was talking to herself or to him. "It feels so hard, but it also feels like…" She seemed to be searching for a word. "Velvet."

Her eyes lifted to his face briefly and he knew she was talking to him. That she knew he was awake.

Her fingers grew a bit bolder in their exploration, and his heart stopped as she cupped his balls, rolling them slightly in her hand.

"These, however, feel so delicate, I'm scared I'm going to break them." She rubbed her cheek on his length. "How can something so hard be so soft?"

"I-I don't know," he groaned. Did she know she was killing him? How much people in the last hundred years would have paid to see him lying in a bed sweating, as this innocent girl tortured him.

His fists gripped handfuls of sheets. He didn't care if he shredded them. His gaze returned to Melissa when her tongue swept over the head of his cock.

"Mmmm. That tasted nice." His eyes rolled into the back of his head as her mouth began to suck on the tip of his cock before slowly releasing it. "Tell me what to do."

"You're doing a damn good job on your own, Angel," he forced out. No. She was killing him. Fuck Chinese water torture—Melissa's innocent exploration would have him confessing any sin in no time.

"No, I just got tired of waiting for you to wake up. And I figured you'd try to stop me. Duncan, I want to do this. Tell me? Please?"

Was there anything in this world he would deny her? Even without her mouth so close to his cock, he knew he'd have done anything she wanted.

Releasing a fistful of sheet, he placed his hand over hers. "Wrap your hand around it." She complied instantly. Guiding her hand up and down his cock, Duncan groaned. "That feels really nice."

"What else?" she asked after a few minutes of matching his rhythm.

Gods, could he handle her doing anything else?

He released her hand, his hips flexing slightly as she continued stroking him on her own. His finger traced her lips as he looked into her eyes. "Angel, I won't ask you to do that—"

She didn't give him a chance to finish. "Just tell me if I'm doing it wrong, okay?" Without pausing so he could protest he felt her mouth replacing her hand on his cock. Her teeth grazed against his skin slightly.

Duncan's fingers combed through her hair, toying with the long strands. It took all of his control to prevent him from wrapping her hair around his hand and thrusting up into her mouth. When her finger began to trace his balls he groaned.

"I'm sorry, did I hurt you?" she asked, pulling back slightly.

"No, Angel, it felt really, really good."

She nodded as her mouth covered him once again.

He didn't want to be rough with her, he wanted to be able to go slow and make sure she wasn't hurt, but his hips wouldn't remain still. He arched into her mouth. Instead of pulling away, Melissa matched his pace.

He was going to come. "Oh gods Angel, I'm gonna come. If you want to pull back, you really should now..." he warned, his voice thick and hoarse. He didn't want her to stop, but he wouldn't be a dick and just shoot his load into her mouth without warning either. To his delight, she continued to suck him into her mouth, her movements more demanding.

He fought it as long as he could. When he came, she focused on the head of his cock, taking everything he had to offer.

His orgasm hit so hard he was left weak and trembling, much as she had been before they went to sleep.

Her mouth gave one more hard tug on his cock before she gently returned him to his shorts and laid her head on his stomach.

"That was nice. I think I understand what you meant last night, about giving pleasure."

Nice? Hell, he had seen heaven, touched it!

He pulled her up his body, pleased that she hadn't gotten dressed yet. "Melissa, why did you..."

"Because I wanted to."

"I didn't expect..."

"I know." She placed a gentle kiss on his lips before snuggling her head on his shoulder. "That's part of why I wanted to. And if you don't mind, I think I'd like to try it again sometime."

"Are you trying to kill me?" he groaned.

"You didn't like it?"

Duncan tried to make her look him in the eye, but she avoided him. Rolling so she was pinned beneath him, he turned her face. "No, Angel. I never thought a bastard like me would ever be able to even hope for a glimpse of paradise. You gave that to me today." He flexed against her, his cock already growing hard again. "*You* do this to me. Just the thought of feeling your mouth around me again makes me hard as a rock. But I'm so damned scared of hurting you."

"You won't hurt me." She sounded so sure, so confident in him.

"I might," he told her. "I like to get rough sometimes."

"And I'm not made of glass." She kissed his cheek then began to nibble on his ear. Her arms locked around his neck, holding him close. "So, when do I get to do that again?"

Lying beneath him, his taste still in her mouth, Melissa wanted him even more than she had the previous night. She wanted to feel his tongue in her mouth, to feel him inside of her body. But she wouldn't push him. She wasn't sure if he would want to kiss her after she'd just given him a blow job. She remembered more conversations from the girl's locker room. The girls that got around were always giving everyone else advice. And one of the things they'd stressed was that guys hated to be kissed after you blew them.

She continued nibbling on his shoulder, her body aching for more.

He tilted her head gently, and sucked on her lower lip. "You don't want to kiss me anymore?" he teased.

"I thought maybe you didn't want—that you wouldn't want to taste…"

His lips descended on hers, his tongue thrusting into her mouth. Melissa's fingers curved as they moved over his back. Her hips arched against him. She couldn't remember wrapping her legs around his waist, but forced herself to release him. Tugging his boxers down his ass, she kept him distracted by sucking on his tongue and teasing his fangs.

Slowly and carefully she felt his cock against her bare hand as she stroked him, her foot pulling the underwear down to his knees.

"What are you up to?" Duncan asked against her cheek.

"I just want to feel all of you," she told him. He chuckled but didn't stop her, instead he helped her to finish pulling the shorts off.

He returned to her, an eyebrow arched. She didn't give him time to begin questioning her again. Lifting her head slightly, she bit down on his ear, smiling when he growled against her neck. She felt his mouth tugging on her flesh and allowed him free access to her.

Still stroking his cock with her hand she slid it between her nether lips, arching as it rubbed against her clit.

"Melissa…" He rolled, placing himself beneath her. His hands covered her breasts, thumbs rubbing against her nipples.

Moisture dripped from her, and she knew the time was right. She wouldn't give him the opportunity to deny her again. Lifting herself slightly, she positioned him then dropped down.

Pain filled her body, and all the desire vanished as she felt as though she'd been ripped apart. A few rogue tears rolled down her cheek.

"Gods, Melissa…" Duncan said, pain filling his voice. Had she hurt him too? When he tried to move she cried out. "Shh, Angel. Please trust me?"

Her eyes closed against the pain, she nodded once.

"This might hurt a little." He adjusted slowly until she was beside him then held perfectly still.

The area between her legs was throbbing. How could anyone find this pleasurable? How could it be so different from what she felt earlier?

Feeling brave enough to crack her eyes open slightly, she saw him watching her. He pressed his lips against hers, slowly, tenderly. "Oh Angel." He kissed her gently again.

"You didn't feel this big in my mouth," she whispered. "I just thought…"

"It's all right. I promise you, Angel, the pain will end." She attempted to look at him but he looked so blurry. "Melissa, I'm going to bite you. I want that link to you. Will you let me bite you?"

Shifting awkwardly beside him, she cried out as pain filled her again. Closing her eyes, she agreed, her teeth clenched against the pain.

"Mel, Angel, stop. I want you to look at me." She shook her head, squeezing her eyes closed even tighter. "Melissa, look at me," he demanded. The tone was so different from what he always used around her that she instantly complied. Looking into his gray eyes, she saw him move closer.

C820

She was wrapped so tightly around him, his body wanted to move, to thrust deep into her, but he refused to cause her one more second of pain than absolutely necessary. He berated himself for not predicting she would try that. Each whimper from her made him berate himself even more.

Staring into her eyes, Duncan sucked her lower lip into his mouth nibbling on it, allowing her to feel his fangs on her as his suckling grew slowly stronger. Laving her lip with his tongue with each pass, he managed to scratch the inside of her lip without her noticing before he closed the wound. When she didn't try to stop him, he continued. Trailing down to her neck, he began to gently suckle her, just above her shoulder.

After about thirty seconds, his mouth grew harder, more insistent. Adding in his teeth slightly, he nipped her flesh.

Melissa wrapped her arms around him, gripping his flesh. Even her legs lost some of the tension in them, but he remained still. *Good. She's relaxing slightly.* Giving one final pull he decided it was time. His mouth became demanding, sucking on her flesh hard as his fangs slid into her, then withdrew quickly.

He allowed the blood to flow into his mouth. After taking several sips he closed the wound with a swipe of his tongue, hoping he hadn't caused her more pain.

Reaching out tentatively, he slipped into her mind.

Oh gods, it hurts.

Duncan shifted slightly, trying to hold her as close as possible without hurting her.

No. No, don't move, please don't move, she whimpered.

He kissed a path to her ear, nipping it sharply, but not drawing blood. Melissa's nails dug slightly into his back and a brief moan filled her head.

He toyed with her ear for a few more seconds before kissing her. His tongue slid into her mouth, coaxing hers to come out to play. One of his hands traveled up her side, cupping her breast, thumb teasing her nipple.

Gods that feels nice. Please keep doing that, it feels good.

He wasn't sure if she was trying to speak to him or if she was too wrapped up in the sensations surrounding her body. Either way, he was more than grateful for link between them. Using her thoughts to guide him, Duncan moved slowly.

He continued to knead her breast as he leaned closer to kiss her. His mouth gentle, he nipped at her lips until she opened to him.

Mmmm, I love it when he does that with his tongue, she thought as his tongue slid over hers.

He did it again and this time he heard her moan with his ears as well as inside of her mind.

Slowly the desire built within her once again. He could feel Melissa growing wetter around him and bit down on his tongue to prevent himself from rushing forward. Angling a hand between their bodies, he found her clit. There was a brief flash of panic in her mind and her eyes flew open, but then she was quickly moaning again. He pinched and tugged on her clit, reveling in the pleasure he heard in her thoughts. Her hips began to thrust minutely and he had to force back his own groan.

Faster, she pleaded in her thoughts and he complied. When the orgasm ripped through her body, Duncan was shocked with the intensity of it. He felt her pussy contracting around him, making his cock ache to plunge into her.

Gathering her in his arms, he rolled onto his back as the pleasure still coursed through her body. When the tremors began to ease, she opened her eyes and he could see the shock on her face as she looked down at him.

Sandy Lynn

How the hell... "How? When? Why didn't it hurt?"

"Oh, Angel." He gave a thick chuckle. His balls were beginning to ache with the need to push into her, but still he forced himself to remain still.

"So what happens now?"

"That depends on you. Are you still in pain?"

Melissa shook her head tentatively, "I don't think so."

Finding reassurance inside her mind, and unable to feel any traces of pain or panic, he closed the link. His heart—the one most people he met swore he didn't have—began to ache now that he couldn't feel her so completely any longer. But he refused to simply force his way into her head.

Placing his hands on her hips, he told her seriously, "Tell me if it hurts."

"You're gonna move? But I thought we... I thought it..." He could see the fear in her eyes.

"No, Angel, you are. Love, you're in control."

"But I don't know what to do."

"I'll help you. Have you ever ridden a horse?" She shook her head. "Another thing we shall have to change." He smiled. "Begin raising yourself to your knees." Melissa obeyed and he began to slide out of her. "Now, back down." She looked at him as though he were insane, but complied, slowly.

"It doesn't hurt." Amazement colored her voice.

Then why do I feel like I'm about to die? Duncan groaned inside his head. His hands remained on her hips, gently guiding her movements as she explored the new sensations. He gritted his teeth, bit his tongue and the inside of his cheek—did anything he could think of to prevent himself from taking control, slamming into her until he shot his come deep into her.

"This feels really nice," Melissa told him, still slowly sliding up and down his cock.

He tried to smile, tried to say something reassuring, but he was scared that if he stopped concentrating for one second, he wouldn't be able to control himself with her any longer. She'd already experienced more pain than he had hoped, he refused to do that to her as well.

114

"Are you all right? Am I hurting you?"

"No, love, you aren't," he told her, teeth still clenched.

"You look like you're in pain." She stopped moving, eliciting a growl from him. His teeth were elongated and he couldn't help the almost feral expression on his face.

Melissa watched as Duncan's eyes narrowed and she got a glimpse of his teeth between his parted lips. She supposed to some he would be terrifying. But she couldn't help smiling. She could never be afraid of the man that had just done so much to ease her pain.

"Fuck me, Duncan."

"We were—"

"No. I want you to fuck me. I want to feel you on top of me, like before. I want to feel your arms around me, your mouth on me."

"You don't know what you're asking of me. Angel, I'll hurt you."

"No, you won't. I will never believe you would ever hurt me. Please?" As an afterthought she added, "I promise to let you know if it hurts."

She stared at him a moment, careful to stay perfectly still no matter how badly her body wanted to move. When he nodded, she lowered to kiss him, her hair forming a curtain around them.

He wrapped his arms tightly around her, one hand holding the back of her head, forcing her to remain in their kiss. Lightning fast, she felt the bed beneath her, and Duncan's weight pressing into her. Wrapping her legs around his waist, she moaned into their kiss.

"Angel, I don't want to hurt—"

She cut him off with a kiss. "You won't." She placed a gentle kiss on his forehead then sucked his lower lip into her mouth and released it. "Show me the stars?"

He devoured her mouth in response as his body began to withdraw from hers. He thrust into her, and Melissa wrapped the sensations around her. She felt his mouth tugging on her neck, the same spot he'd bit her before. Her entire body began to tense as his thrusts became harder, faster, his mouth matching the frantic pace.

"Drink," she gasped.

A sharp pain in her neck heightened her pleasure rather than detracted from it. Beneath closed lids her eyes rolled up into her head. Her fingers dug into his flesh, and a scream ripped from her throat as she was pushed over the edge into an orgasm more intense than the last. As her body trembled she could feel him push into her one, two more times before his body stilled and he growled into her neck.

His tongue closed the wound on her neck and he placed a kiss against the mark. All of his weight rested on her, but she welcomed it. Melissa never wanted to move, she never wanted to leave this room or Duncan's embrace.

He tried to roll off her, to pull away, but she refused to release him. "Stay," she asked.

"I'm crushing you."

"Yeah, but I like it."

He chuckled and moved them so they were side by side. Melissa pouted at his loss and he bit lightly on her lip.

"I'm sorry you were in so much pain." His playful manner was gone instantly.

"I don't remember that." Looking into his eyes she smiled, tracing his lips with her forefinger. "What I will always remember about tonight is how the man I loved was patient and gentle, and bit the hell out of his tongue just to make sure it was special for me."

"Oh, Angel, you deserved more. You deserved roses and candlelight and chocolate, and all that romantic shit I suck at."

"If I had the choice to do it all over again, the night you described or what we did, there's no contest. Duncan, I would gladly suffer any amount of pain to be able to feel what I felt with you."

"Why do you have such faith in me? Gods know I've never done anything in my entire life to deserve it. I'm not a good man. I'm a killer. Mel, you deserve someone who—"

She stopped him. "My trust is not easily given, Duncan. It's the most precious thing I have. I don't care who you are around anyone else. I know in my heart that you will never hurt me. And quite honestly, that's all that matters. I won't listen to you trying to convince me that you're a bad man. I'll never believe that you would ever hurt me."

"Angel…"

"I know we may not be forever, Duncan. I'm okay with that," she lied, praying he wasn't inside her mind at that moment. "But while we are together, I want you to know one very important thing."

"And what's that?" He smiled.

"If you ever badmouth yourself to me again, I will get out of this bed, go upstairs, get a knife and stab you."

He laughed, pulling her close. "Quite the violent little thing, aren't you?"

"I have a lot of pent up aggression. Want to help me work some off?" she flirted.

"Aren't you sore?"

"A little. But if you're not interested…" Melissa began to rise from the bed but Duncan pulled her back down to him.

Lounging half on top of him, she laughed as he tickled her sides. All playfulness left when she stared in his eyes, her heart filled with love. Their kiss was frantic, as though neither could get enough of the other.

Chapter Ten

"Mel?"

Melissa had just stepped out of the shower when she heard her brother calling. Quickly wrapping her body in a bathrobe, and winding a towel around her hair, she went to the door to answer him.

"Coming," she called back. Taking a look in the mirror to assure herself that she didn't look any different, she prepared herself to see him. Walking out of the bathroom, she slowly walked down the stairs, following her brother's voice. "What's up?" she asked casually. "Why aren't you at La's? You two didn't fight did you?"

"I'm meeting her at the club. I haven't seen you at CS lately."

"I've only been gone a few nights." She shrugged, walking past him to get water from the fridge.

"Four."

"I'm sorry?"

"Not counting the night you disappeared, you've been gone four nights. This isn't like you. You're not still worried about *him* are you?"

"No, Gareth. Honestly I haven't thought about him in days. I've just been a little, preoccupied..."

His eyes narrowed as she shifted, her fingers playing with the bottle cap.

"Mel, I'm gonna find out what happened. You can tell me or..." Gareth shrugged.

Oh dear gods no. "You wouldn't."

"You know I will."

"You're a big bully."

"I'm looking out for my little sister. Tell me what's been going on."

"Now, Gareth, calm down," she said, trying to make her voice soothing as she backed slowly from him. She would never be afraid of him, but the last thing she needed was him inside her head. "I've been seeing this guy I met—"

Gareth roared. "Who is he? I want to know who the fuck he is right now."

"Gareth…" She tried to placate him.

"I want to meet him, Mel. I want to meet him and let him know that if he lays a finger on you, my face is the last thing he'll see in this life."

She sighed, her fingers pressing against her temple. "I'm not a child," she told him softly.

"I know you're not a child," her brother yelled. "How serious are things between you two?"

Melissa looked away from him, her head tilting slightly to cover the side of her neck that still held Duncan's mark. She didn't want Gareth to know what they had been doing, but she wouldn't lie to him either.

A second later she felt a hand turning her head and pulling the bathrobe from her neck.

"I'll kill him. Who is he? He's a dead man. What's his name Melissa?"

"You think I'll tell you now? I won't let you go bully him," she screamed back.

"You're my sister," Gareth yelled. "I don't want some guy treating you like you're a—" He froze mid-sentence.

"Oh no, please, finish that thought. You don't want some guy treating me like I'm what? A woman? A whore? What?"

"I don't want you to get hurt. That's all I've ever wanted." His head bowed slightly, he left the room.

Setting the bottle down on the counter, she left the kitchen. She found him easily, sitting in the living room on the couch, head still lowered in defeat.

Melissa sat down next to him, laying her head on his shoulder, the way she had done so often when she was younger.

"When did you grow up? I look at you and I can't believe the woman you've turned into. When did this happen? Why didn't anyone tell me? When did you stop being fourteen?"

"Gareth, I'm always going to be your little sister. I'm always going to love you and you will always be my hero. But I'm not a little girl anymore."

"Does he treat you right?" Gareth's voice was soft.

"I wouldn't be with him if he didn't." Her brother's arm circled her shoulders.

"Will I ever get to meet him?"

"Yes."

"Can I still kill him if he hurts you?"

She chuckled. "Maybe."

"Maybe." He looked at her and Melissa could feel the love and concern radiating off him. "Is he... Is he vampire?"

She looked at him skeptically. "Do you really want to know?"

"No. But tell me anyway."

"He is. And yes, I've let him drink from me," she told him before he could ask what she knew would be his next question.

"Gods, I did not need to know that. So you really trust him, huh?"

"Yes, Gareth, I do."

"Do you love him?"

"With all my heart. I don't think I've ever met a more wonderful man. He listens to me, really listens. He doesn't pressure me to do anything I don't want. He's a great guy. The second greatest man I've had the honor of meeting."

"Second?" he asked in a quiet voice. To others he was the ultimate alpha male. But around Melissa, he was simply her brother. They couldn't have been more related if they'd had the same parents. And just as he'd reassured her about his love for her so recently, she was more than willing to do the same for him.

"Yes, the second. Gareth, you will always be the first man I've ever met who gave me any hope that all men weren't like my stepfather. You are the greatest man I know, but there is room in my heart for both of you."

"I know, Mel. I'm just not used to the idea of sharing you. I don't think I like it."

She laughed. "You don't have to like it."

"But I have to accept it," he finished the familiar phrase. "Can we do something tonight? Just you and me, like we used to do in the old days, before you were all grown up?"

"I'd like that."

"Are you too old for dinner, a movie, and miniature golf?"

"Not if you throw in a couple of laps around the Go-Kart track."

"Deal."

Melissa climbed off the couch and headed to change.

"Gareth?"

"Yes?"

"Don't think just by buying me supper you can get out of buying me a large popcorn and candy."

She heard him chuckle. "You never let me get away with it before, I wouldn't expect you to start now."

"I love you."

"I love you, too, Mel."

CB&O

Melissa looked at her reflection in the mirror. Had she ever looked happy? Her gaze moved down to her cheek. The bruise was finally gone.

She'd been careful not to do anything that would provoke her stepfather, given him no reason to slap her for the last week.

Her gaze traveled to the bags under her eyes. Pulling out the makeup her former best friend had given her for her birthday, she began to conceal the shadows on her face. Sleep had become a luxury she couldn't afford since her stepfather had begun to come to her room at night. She wouldn't hear him approach, she'd only look up, stretching as she was about to prepare for bed and see him there, staring at her from the doorway—always staring at her.

Instead of getting much needed sleep, she would simply open a different textbook, as though she'd only just finished with the one subject. At some point he would stop staring at her and go to his room. Only when she heard his snores would she allow herself a mere three hours of sleep, always careful to wake up early enough to take a shower before his alarm sounded. She even made sure to have breakfast on the table. When he left for work, she would finally repack her backpack and apply the camouflaging makeup before going to school.

She was beginning to look much older than her age. She wondered if she would ever again feel carefree? Should she ask for help at school? Not from the staff—never from them. They'd already proven whose side they were on. She thought about the guy in her English class, Ben. When she'd first begun to look tired, he approached her, asking if she wanted something to help her stay awake.

At the time she had declined. Her mom would never understand if she turned to drugs. Her eyes welled with familiar tears. Quickly blinking them back, Melissa shook her head. She couldn't go down that road, couldn't think of her mother. There wasn't enough time to reapply her makeup.

Looking at her reflection she wondered if she should take Ben up on his offer. Surely becoming an addict was better than this. It had to be better than this constant fear of what would happen if she fell asleep and her stepfather walked into her room. It had to be better than the pain inside her all the time, better than aching to see her mother again, than feeling she couldn't talk to anyone. Sweet oblivion would be better than feeling as though she were a shadow walking through the world. Something that no one noticed anymore, that no one cared about, and, more importantly, that no one would miss.

Her gaze lowered to the razor her stepfather used to shave. It would be so easy to give up. So easy to run a nice hot bath. By the time the school would be able to get in touch with her stepfather to report her absence, it would be too late. She'd be free of him, free of people who swore they cared about her, then turned their backs. Free of people who looked through her...

Picking up the old-fashioned razor, she carefully removed the dull blade. Concentrating on how easy it would be, how nice it would be, how happy she'd be to see her mother, she placed the edge against the flesh of her wrist, where the blue vein began. Applying a slight pressure, Melissa fought back a cry as it dug into her flesh.

No. Something inside of her screamed as the first pregnant drop of blood appeared.

Dropping the blade as though it had grown red-hot in her grip, she quickly grabbed her backpack and ran out of the house to the bus stop. All day she avoided looking anyone in the face. Her former best friend, Kate, approached her at lunch, but Melissa couldn't even look her in the eyes, she refused to speak to the other girl. She was just so tired of hurting. And she would never, ever take the chance of her stepfather approaching Kate. She cared about her friend too much to risk that happening. She'd rather lose the best friend she'd ever had than see pity in her eyes when she looked at her. And pity would be there once Kate learned what was truly happening when Melissa got home from school everyday.

Besides, she tried to comfort herself. *What could Kate do? She'd just tell her parents, they'd call the cops, and they would all believe Travis.*

Maybe Melissa would be able to escape for a short time to a hospital, but more likely she would only become drugged. Then what chance would she have against him? They'd dismiss her fears as irrational since he never acted like anything but a caring guardian around witnesses.

"What proof do you have that he plans to hurt you?" they would ask.

Her only proof was his stares. Stares that told her he did not see her as a child. Stares that told her he was only waiting for the chance to corner her...

"Have you reconsidered?" The question jerked her back to the lunch-room.

"Ben, I don't...I can't...I can't afford them," she admitted quietly. She might not be able to commit suicide, but perhaps she could kill herself indirectly.

He sat down beside her. "Here, this one's on me." He pressed something into her hand, her fist closed automatically around it. "And next time, I'm sure we can work something out." His hand rested on her knee.

"I don't understand."

Ben's hand moved up her thigh. "You are a beautiful girl, Melissa. If you and I were *together*, I'd make sure you had what you need, anything you wanted." He leaned in and kissed her lips. Though he was a handsome guy, she felt nothing.

"Think about it," he told her, pulling back. "You take those, and think about what I said. I'll make sure I'm in English class all week, if you want to take me up on my offer."

Waiting until he left the table, Melissa put the drugs into her backpack. She didn't try to find out what he'd handed her. She didn't care. She finally had another option, something that would hopefully dull the pain she felt constantly.

The school day passed quickly. When she got home, she was surprised to see her stepfather sitting on the couch waiting for her.

"Sit down, we need to talk."

Hesitantly, moving against her better judgment, she followed his orders, not wanting to give him a reason to hit her.

"You've been spending too much time studying."

"I-I want to make sure I get into a good college."

"That's fine, but it's been interfering with things that are a little more important right now. You haven't been sleeping. Don't think I don't know this. And don't think your teachers haven't called me about the sudden change in attitude from you. They think you're on drugs. Are you, Melissa? Are you doing drugs?"

"No."

"Don't lie to me." He lifted his hand as though he were about to slap her. Without thought, Melissa cowered, trying to shield her face.

"No. I haven't, I swear."

"Good." He smirked. She wasn't sure if he was pleased she wasn't doing drugs or by her instant cowering. Though she suspected it was the latter.

"Now. Things are going to change around here. This is what's going to happen. From now on, you have from the time you get home from school until I get home to study. I still expect to come home to a clean house, and supper waiting on the table. I'll go to the bar, and you can watch TV, or study, after you finish cleaning up. When I get home you *will* be in bed." His hand moved from its position on the back of the couch, to her thigh. "Do not make me come for you tonight, or you will regret it."

Fighting back the bile that rose in her throat, she nodded her understanding. She felt an immediate need for a shower to clean away his touch, the taint he had placed on her soul with his suggestion.

"Good girl. I always knew you were smart. I'll be back in about an hour. When I get back, you better be ready."

Acknowledging his words once again, Melissa stood, grabbing her backpack from the floor. Tears of horror filled her eyes as he slapped her butt. She practically ran to her bedroom where she put her bag down beside her bed, in its usual spot. Waiting until she heard the front door shut, she opened her closet. She felt around until she found the loose floorboard she used for a hiding place. Ignoring the diary she used to write in, before her life became a giant nightmare she continued searching the secret spot.

Picking up an old wallet of her mothers, she glanced inside. She had been saving up to buy her mother something nice for Christmas. But now, she had a different purpose for it. Melissa tucked the wallet safely in her back pocket.

Finished gathering up the few things she planned to take with her, she headed for the kitchen to fix herself a sandwich. Quickly choking it down she tried to casually walk out of the house. She forced herself to keep her pace slow and easy as she walked down the street and waited for the bus. When it arrived, she got on, like she was only going to run an errand or two, knowing that none of the neighbors would see anything unusual about this. Heck, they thought it was great that she "pitched in" so much to help Travis out.

Instead she went downtown and walked around, as though she didn't have a care in the world. When she got hungry she walked into a fast food place and bought something to eat. When she grew tired she looked for a place that would hide her from onlookers.

Her money lasted almost a week. When she didn't have any left she considered going home. Maybe she could go to Kate's house? Maybe Kate would protect her? No, her parents would send her home insisting that Travis was worried sick. Ben? She didn't know where or how to find him.

Thinking about it most of the day, she decided she had three options. She could go home—where she knew Travis would be beyond pissed, she could make some money, or she could show up at school and pray she could find Ben before the teachers reported her sudden reappearance.

Every choice would involve some man using her body. Looking around, she knew she'd prefer to sell her body than her soul. And going to either Travis or Ben she'd lose both.

Taking a deep breath, she walked through the streets, trying to gather enough courage to follow her plan through. If she couldn't follow her plan that night, she'd go for plan b—Ben.

"Excuse me," a handsome brown-haired man said when she bumped into him.

Remembering every movie or television show she'd ever seen, she smiled up at him. "Looking for a good time?" She pasted what she hoped was a sexy smile, a sexy look on her face.

The man's eyes widened in shock. "You can't be more than... Where's your family?"

"Never mind," Melissa said, feeling completely incompetent. To her embarrassment, her stomach growled as she turned to walk away.

Reaching out, the man stopped her. "How about you and I go get something to eat?"

"No thanks." Looking at him, she decided she couldn't chance him taking her to the police.

"Come on. There's a little place right down the street. My treat." Her stomach began to rumble again, tightening as she felt the effects of going without food since the previous day. "I know you're hungry." She still just stood, staring at him. "Come on, if you were willing to 'show me a good time', surely you're willing to sit across from me and have a simple conversation."

Reluctantly she agreed, unsure when she would be able to eat next.

They walked to the diner in silence. When they sat down, the man sat across from her. He ordered bottled water and nothing else. With a smile he said, "Order whatever you like."

She ordered a hamburger and onion rings.

"So, what's your name?"

"It's not that I don't appreciate this, but why are you being nice to me. You want me to go with you after I eat? I'm fine with that," she quickly added.

"Nope, just want to talk. It's been a while since I got to sit down over a meal and have a decent conversation."

She watched him suspiciously, but didn't move. When the food was put in front of her, it took all her willpower not to simply shove the food down her throat.

"How long have you been on the street?"

"A week," she told him between large bites. When Melissa looked up, she saw him nod thoughtfully.

"My name is Gareth." He held his hand out. She wiped her hand on a napkin then shook it.

"Pleasure to meet you. I'm Melissa."

"Melissa, a beautiful name for a beautiful girl." He was quiet as she continued to eat her food. After a short while he asked, "Where's your family, Melissa?"

"Thank you for the food. I should probably let you get back to your life. I've taken enough of your time."

"You haven't had dessert yet." He motioned for the waitress and ordered the biggest slice of apple pie they had.

Looking into his eyes, not understanding what she was searching for, she asked, "Why are you being so nice to me?"

"Because, Melissa, no one should ever feel like they don't have anywhere to turn. Especially not someone so young. You're far too young to be forced to depend on yourself for everything you need."

Tears filled her eyes and she quickly rubbed them away, trying to maintain the tough-girl persona she'd had to adopt since she ran away. As the pie was set in front of her, she was able to eat at a slower pace, thankful that her stomach was no longer in knots.

"What happened?"

"I ran away from home. Things are…I don't belong there."

"Home is the one place we all do belong. Whatever happened, I'm sure things will blow over. Would you really prefer to make your home on the street?" His voice was hypnotic. It allowed her to finally admit to herself that she was scared. "Would you like me to walk with you?"

She nodded. If she could get home, and make it to Kate or Ben's, she wouldn't be alone. She just didn't want to be left alone in the dark anymore, where boxes had glowing eyes and squeaked. Or visions of her stepfather jumped out at her from every shadow. Even there in the dark, in the middle of the city where he couldn't find her, she had nightmares about the things that could happen to a single girl in the dark.

As they walked, Gareth continued to ask her questions in his calming voice. While she didn't volunteer any information, it did become easier to talk to him. She told him her mother had died not long ago and that it was just her and her stepfather at home. She told him about school, how much she studied and her dreams to go to a college far away from there.

All too soon they were standing in front of her house. The white paint was chipping and sorely in need of attention. Melissa felt a wave of embarrassment wash over her as Gareth looked at the house. She began to walk up the path to the front door and was relieved when she heard him follow her. If Travis was there, at least he wouldn't make a scene in front of the kind stranger.

Opening the door, Melissa felt a wave of revulsion sweep over her as she looked at the filth thrown around the room. Dirty clothes were scattered everywhere. She could smell the trash can they kept in the kitchen from the door and there were fast food wrappers, cans, and beer bottles everywhere there was space. The place looked as though she'd been gone for a month not a mere week.

When she saw the expression on her stepfather's face, her fear rose, paralyzing her. *He won't hit me in front of a witness. He won't hit me in front of a witness. He won't hit me in front of a witness.* Over and over she repeated the litany, trying to convince herself it was true.

To her shock he pulled his hand back and slapped her, full force across the face. Freed from her terror, her body fell to the floor.

"How dare you leave me? Look at this mess. How can you expect me to live like this? This dump isn't fit for a pig to live in. I expect this house to be spotless before I get home tomorrow."

Curling into a ball she looked up at him, her hand covering her throbbing cheek, trying to protect the sensitive flesh from another blow.

Gareth made a low sound in his throat that got Travis's attention. He stepped closer to where her body had landed and snarled. "How dare you whore yourself out to the first man you meet. Your mama was a whore, too. I shouldn't be surprised you followed in her footsteps."

She wanted to scream. She wanted to defend her mother but past experience told her that would only be rewarded with more, much harder smacks. Instead she hid her face, trying to protect her head from the worst of

Sandy Lynn

the blows. Tears ran down her cheeks as she kept her mouth shut, too afraid of the pain to defend the mother she had loved so much. She felt like a coward, like she didn't deserve to have even the memory of her mother, but she wasn't sure she would survive another full beating from Travis.

When the blow never came, she looked up again and saw him dangling three feet off the floor as Gareth gripped him by the throat. Gareth's teeth, so normal as he had spoken gently to her, coaxing her to return home, were now long and sharp. They looked incredibly lethal, like in the vampire movies she and her mother used to watch all the time before she got sick. For a second she wished he would kill Travis.

"If you touch her again there will be hell to pay." He threw Travis through the open doorway to the kitchen and Melissa could hear him hit the wall.

Crawling to the corner, she curled into a ball once again, intending to be as far out of reach as possible when Travis returned. Perhaps he wouldn't even notice her, and just leave for the bar.

"Don't be afraid of me, little one," Gareth told her, looking down. His fangs gleamed dangerously in the light, but she couldn't muster enough fear to be afraid of him as well as the monster she knew. Not when he'd shown her nothing but kindness, and even protected her. "I promise you have nothing to fear from me. You never need to fear me."

Her control broke. "Please don't leave. Please. I'm not afraid of you, I swear," she told him honestly, easily begging him. "Please stay. He's going to beat me when you leave." Her sobs grew stronger. She didn't care that she was begging a perfect stranger. She didn't care what he asked for in return for defending her. He could have her body, he could have her blood, he could have her soul! She just didn't want to be left alone with Travis any longer. "He's going to be so far beyond pissed that someone protected me." Hugging her knees she tried to become a smaller target. "It's why I ran away... Please don't leave me," she sobbed into her knees.

Gareth pulled away from her slightly. "Little one, I must leave." His voice was filled with remorse. "But I will return tomorrow night. I swear on my honor, by the gods, I will return for you tomorrow night." He turned away
130

from her and when she followed his line of vision she saw her stepfather propping himself up with a wall as he stood in the doorway. "If you harm one single hair on this child's head while I am gone, I promise you whatever hell you believe exists will become a paradise compared to what I will do to you."

A small grain of hope sparked to life within her. Could he mean what he said? He certainly sounded like he did. But she was so scared to feel hope, so scared she would be disappointed yet again.

As she watched, Gareth approached him. Leaning down, it looked as though he were giving Travis a kiss on the neck. He straightened and Melissa could see a few drops of blood on his lip before he licked them away. "I *will* be back tomorrow night. Eight sharp, when I arrive, you *will* sign papers giving me full custody of this child. If you refuse, I will make you wish you were never born. I will make you beg me to allow you to sign those papers. Have I made myself clear?"

Travis nodded dumbly, his hand going to his neck, where there was no visible sign of any wound. Not even a bruise.

"And just so you don't try to run, I've tasted you. I will be able to find you wherever you go." Gareth returned to Melissa, kneeling down as though he didn't care about the filth around him ruining his beautiful clothes. When he spoke, his tone was gentle once again. "I will be back for you tomorrow night. Pack only what you want to take with you, whatever has any special meaning for you. I will provide you with everything you'll ever need." He turned his head and his voice dripped with contempt. "And if he so much as raises his voice to you, tell me when I return and he will pay for it."

"You're going to believe whatever that little bitch tells you?" Travis was clearly panicking.

"I will *always* believe whatever my little sister tells me. So I suggest you be *very* careful in how you treat her while I am gone." With a final reassuring look, Gareth left the house.

Not waiting for Travis's reaction, Melissa flew to her room, angling a chair underneath the knob to prevent him from getting inside.

Please, please God, let him have meant what he said, she prayed as she rested all of her weight against the door. The front door slammed and Melissa finally allowed herself to relax slightly. She wanted more than anything to take a shower, to get clean after her extended stay downtown, but decided she would rather wait one more day. After what had happened tonight, if Gareth didn't come for her, she was sure the mortician wouldn't care if she smelled of body sweat or coconuts.

Walking around her room, she gathered up the few items that carried special memories for her. The jewelry she had been given by her mother, a sweater her mom had loved seeing her in, the teddy bear that had grieved with her, her diary, and her mother's pillowcase. Finally, she grabbed the last letter her mother had ever written to her, the one the nurse handed to her when Melissa found out about her death. It was the last thing her mother would ever write to her, apologizing for her deception. Her meager possessions were placed carefully in her backpack, her notebooks and textbooks taken out.

Outside, the night sky grew lighter as the sun rose. Hugging her knees, she spoke aloud as she rocked back and forth, unsure if she were praying, but knowing she had to talk to her mother at least one last time. "Please, please let Gareth return for me. Mom, I love you so much, and I'm sorry if this makes you sad, but I can't stay here. I swear I'll give him my soul if he asks for it. I'm so sorry, but I'll give him anything he wants if he takes me away from Travis. I miss you so much mommy. I miss you so much and I'll never stop loving you, but I can't stay here. I can't stay here any longer. I can't."

Cʒᙓᴏ

Duncan's eyes jerked open as he felt a tear slide down his arm. In her sleep, Melissa was crying and trembling.

"Shhh, love, you're safe. You're safe here with me." He pressed a kiss to her hair, then another to her neck. Giving a slight whimper, she began to calm as he pulled her tighter against his body and murmured into her ear.

Lying back, he closed his eyes, unable to get the images of her rocking back and forth on her bed out of his mind. No wonder she had problems sleeping. He could still feel her terror, the pain from that bastard's blows. His teeth lengthened, the bloodlust growing deep inside him. Since he'd heard about her stepfather, he'd wondered why Gareth had allowed that bastard to live. Now he knew. Melissa had never told him *exactly* why she ran away. She'd never told him just what the sick fuck was planning to do to her. He was willing to bet any amount of money that to this day Gareth didn't know exactly how bad that *thing*—he refused to call him a man—would have hurt her.

Closing his eyes, he conjured a memory of what her stepfather looked like. If he was ever lucky enough to run into the bastard one night, he swore Travis would feel the pain he inflicted on Melissa tenfold.

Chapter Eleven

Duncan was sitting at a table, thinking about Melissa. It had been just over a week since the first time they made love and two nights since he'd shared her dream. His heart ached for her, but not with pity. In his opinion she was stronger than he had first thought. As he remembered the nightmare he had witnessed through her eyes, he fought to push it aside. If he didn't he would be out in the night, hunting for his prey. And he would guarantee that blonde Melissa had beaten the shit out of would walk away from him with more than a headache. If she was able to walk at all. He fought a growl.

The rage inside of him grew and he quickly shifted his thoughts back to her, to them. Since that first taste, he couldn't seem to get enough of her. He thought about feeling her sweet body beneath his hands. How perfect she felt in his arms, the way she managed to soothe him so completely. Since they had been together he hadn't once felt alone, as though no one would ever be able to accept him.

Staring off into space, he wondered if he could go back to life without her. *No,* his heart screamed, aching at the mere thought of being separated from her.

Would she want to be changed? Would she be willing to go through that for him?

Her brother's a vampire, so at least she knows what would be involved. Will Gareth try to forbid her from changing, or will he be ready to dance with glee?

"Is Bram here yet?"

His thoughts interrupted, he looked up at the woman and smiled. Dani was the perfect complement to Bram. He didn't know much about her other than what he saw on the video screens, but he knew, just from what he saw, that Bram was falling for her. Bram was so caught up in Dani he hadn't been noticing the little things he normally would have spotted immediately. Like the fact that Duncan and Melissa were dating.

"Not yet. Dani, right?" She nodded. "I'm Duncan." He introduced himself. "Would you like me to call him?"

"No, that's alright." She sounded disappointed.

"You're here early." Duncan leaned on the table, making small talk. Something seemed different about her tonight. He had watched the couple together every night that he hadn't been wrapped in Melissa's arms. Watching and waiting for them to realize they each felt the same attraction. It was so obvious in the little things they did. At least, to Duncan, it felt obvious. Something was definitely different tonight. *Could it have something to do with the way she danced with Bram last night?*

"I was just hoping to have a chance to talk to Bram before he got too busy."

Like he wouldn't drop everything for you? Duncan began to stand. "Are you sure you don't want me to call him?" *Bram is gonna be pissed I didn't call him. But maybe it will finally clue him in to how he feels about her...force him to admit it out loud.*

"No, I can wait." Dani sat across from him. The silence stretched out between them. "Do you know what time that woman, um, La I think her name is, usually gets here?" She broke the silence, finally. "You know the one who wears those really skimpy outfits... Last night it was a see-through dress..."

He put her out of her misery. "That's La. They don't usually come until later, why?"

"No reason. I was just wondering if we could have a little girl talk, that's all."

Girl talk? With La? No…Dani is definitely up to something tonight. Before she could stop him, he stood. "I'll call her for you." Quickly walking away, he went to the phone behind the bar and dialed Lalita's number.

"What?" came the grumpy response.

"Hey, La, it's Duncan from CS."

"Oh, hey. Do you know how early it is?" she complained.

"Yeah, but that chick Dani is here, she wants to have some girl talk. I think she wants something else, but that's just me."

He heard La sigh over the phone. "He would have to fall for a human. Okay, tell her I'll be there in about fifteen minutes."

Duncan laughed. "Okay. Thanks, you're a total doll."

"I know." He could hear Lalita's laughter as he hung up the phone and glanced at the clock behind the bar.

On an impulse, he picked up the receiver again and dialed Melissa's number, praying Gareth wouldn't be there.

"Hello?"

Just the sound of her voice put a smile on his face. "Hey gorgeous. What are you doing tonight?"

"Well, I was thinking about going clubbing. Maybe pick up a sexy man and lure him back to my place only to have my wicked way with him."

"Damn, sounds like a good plan. He's one lucky bastard."

"I like it." He could hear the smile in her voice.

"Are you going to come to the club tonight?"

"Maybe," she teased.

He groaned for her, enjoying their game. "Maybe. Angel, you're killing me."

She gave a throaty laugh that went straight to his cock. "You know I'll be there. I can't seem to stay away."

"I'll see you when you get here."

"I'll see you soon, Duncan. I love you." Before he could respond she hung up the phone. She always did that, as though she were afraid to hear his response, or the silence that would follow if he didn't feel the same way.

Motioning to the blonde bartender, he ordered a soda, uncaring that she was the same woman who gave him a show several weeks earlier.

"So, what are you doing later," she asked huskily, her fingers plucking at the neckline of the low-cut top she wore.

"Sorry, I'm busy." Without a second glace at her, Duncan looked at the clock and took the soda back over to Dani.

Placing the drink in front of her he said, "She'll be here in about ten minutes." She looked like she'd swallowed something nasty. He decided she needed to have a little time alone before Lalita arrived. Moving to the shadows, he continued to think about Melissa.

When should he ask her how she felt about being changed? Would she be offended? Happy? Nervous?

As usual his thoughts drifted back to her nightmare. It was unfair of him to know something so intimate about her, something she hadn't volunteered. He felt guilty for having the knowledge, even if he hadn't slipped into her mind consciously. He determined to tell her a bit about his own past, refusing for her to make such an important decision on whether or not she wished to be changed without knowing—truly knowing—what kind of man he was.

Watching from the shadows, he saw Lalita sit down. The two women spoke for a few minutes then disappeared into the back room. They returned to the main room almost immediately with a bag in Dani's hand. Duncan wandered into the back room, for lack of anything else to do now that he'd made his decision to talk about the future with Melissa.

"Gee, you look really busy to me," the bartender said, leaning against the door. Taking a step closer, she slid her hand up her shirt to her breast, cupping the weight in her palm.

"What can I say, I'm a busy guy."

"Do you think you can take time out of your busy schedule to help me out with a small problem?"

He shrugged. "Depends on what you need."

Walking to him slowly, the blonde took his hand and placed it on her breast. "Mmm. That's a really good start."

He pulled his hand back as though burned. "I have a girlfriend."

"That's okay. I'm not looking for a boyfriend. I just want to have a little fun. And I heard that you know how to show a girl one hell of a good time. I've heard some of the other staff call you a freak. It's been entirely too long since I've gotten freaky."

"I don't think you understand." His eyes narrowed. "I'm with someone. I won't cheat on her. I sincerely think you should rethink your choice of playmates, because I'm not playing that game anymore."

"Spoilsport."

"Yup." Duncan left the room without looking back at her. *Let her get herself off*, he thought irritably. Seeing Bram enter the club, he strode purposefully toward his friend. "You just missed Dani."

"She left?"

"Yeah, she grabbed a change of clothes from the back room then she and Lalita left."

"Lalita. You let her leave with Lalita." Bram closed his eyes, a strained expression on his face.

Duncan decided after the irritating blonde bartender, he was up for a little fun. "Looks like our little girl is finally coming out of her shell. That's great, because damn, she's hot. I would never have guessed that she was hiding such a killer body under those baggy clothes..." He saw Bram's hand ball into a fist just before he shoved it behind his back to hide it, but kept his mouth shut about Duncan's comments. *So, you want to play hardball? Yeah, you need to realize you need to make a move on her.* "Do you think she'd go out with me?" He acted like he couldn't sense Bram's discomfort. "When she gets back I think I'm going to ask her out," he continued, as though his friend had agreed he thought she'd go out with him. "Do you think she minds getting a little rough?"

Bram growled low in his throat. "Do what you want," he said through clenched teeth.

Damn, you really have it bad if you haven't noticed I'm with Melissa. "Awesome. You gonna be in the control room later?"

"Yeah."

"Cool." He paused. *Okay, I'll give it one more try, then I'm out of it.* "Maybe I'll follow Gareth's lead and just take Dani to the back room, fuck her brains out there..."

Before he could finish his sentence, Bram had him pinned to the floor, his forearm pressing hard against Duncan's throat. If he were human he'd have been dead from the pressure alone. "If you ever treat Dani like anything other than a lady, you'll be kissing daylight."

"Damn, it's about time. Shit, you know it's kind of fucked up that I even *had* to go there before you laid claim to her. Now will you please stop trying to crush my Adam's apple?" Bram released him, but continued to glare at him. "Every man that works in this place knows she's off-limits, Bram." He clued his friend in as he rubbed his throat. *I hope this heals before Mel sees me. The last thing I need is for her to baby me.* He thought about it for a second. *Then again...*

"But we're just friends."

Yeah, and I'm the pope. He rolled his eyes. "Yeah, right. And how many of your 'friends' have you given unlimited access to the club? Dude, every man here knows that if Dani walks up, no matter if we are closed, she's to be allowed inside, and call you."

"Then why didn't you call me when she got here earlier?" he snapped.

Duncan shrugged. "She didn't want me to. But you were the first thing she asked about."

"I'm a thing, gee, thanks."

I don't have time for this, he growled in his head. "You know what I mean. But, remember, just because *we* all know she's off limits, doesn't mean everyone else knows. Especially when you let her go off and dance with strange men, letting them think they have a chance with her..."

Bram shrugged. "It isn't my place to stop her."

"How clueless can you be?" He tried to keep himself from laughing out loud. "Maybe you *should* go up to the control room. You need to watch that video of you and her dancing, guy. You didn't even dance like that with La…" Shaking his head, he continued. "Go, watch the video. I swear, even though you can see other people dancing around you two, you'd swear you were alone." Duncan walked off, giving him a chance to think about what he said.

Turning discreetly, he saw Bram disappear through the door. Smiling, he walked behind the bar and helped himself to a glass of water.

෴

Melissa arrived at the club. Looking around it was easy to see she'd gotten here early. The majority of the regulars wouldn't be appearing for another few hours.

Hands circled her waist and she began to push her elbow back, intending to jab whoever it was in the stomach before ripping them apart.

"Relax, Angel. It's just me."

Hearing Duncan's voice, she managed to stop herself from hurting him. She hated it when he tricked her into doing it, always felt guilty as hell when she hit him. *Okay*, she silently admitted, *I feel guilty most of the time…*

"Come with me."

"Where are we going?"

"It's a surprise."

She allowed him to lead her over to the bar. To her surprise she saw a door hidden in the shadows just to the side of it. As they passed through it, Bram was entering the club. "I've never noticed that," she said more to herself than to him.

"Most people don't. Which is a good thing." He smiled. Taking her hand, he led her up a set of stairs and through a door on the right.

Looking at the series of screens, Melissa's eyes widened. She'd never guessed they had the place wired with surveillance cameras. Moving from one screen to another she saw the back room and her mouth hung open.

"You can—did you watch—oh. My. Gods." One look back at Duncan, sitting casually in a chair, at the sly smile on his face told her he had watched her brother and La have sex.

He shrugged, his smile never slipping.

"Why did you bring me up here?" She couldn't stop her curiosity. "Do people have sex in that room a lot?"

"I wanted to talk to you. We need to talk."

Oh gods. He's breaking up with me. Her throat closed at the thought. *He's bored with me. He doesn't want someone that's such a wreck. Gods, I'm not good enough in bed. This wasn't supposed to happen so soon. I thought we had at least a few more weeks.* Melissa struggled to keep herself from hyperventilating, amazed when her voice sounded calm. "I'm listening."

"Sit down," he told her, standing.

This is not good. Not good at all. Despite her inner panic she obeyed, sitting on the warm chair.

"There's something I have to tell you, and I hope you understand. It's okay if you don't, but I hope you'll at least hear me out before you comment."

Oh gods, now he's giving me permission to be angry. Who does he think he is, she wondered, anger already blossoming within her. She welcomed the feeling; it felt so much better than the fear and insecurity.

"There's no easy way to say this…"

"Then just say it and let's get this over with," she told him, her voice cold.

Duncan nodded and began. "I know what happened the day you ran away from home. I know what happened while you were on the streets, and how Gareth became your brother."

Of all the things she was expecting to hear from him, that was the last thing on her mind.

141

"You—you snooped through my head?" She couldn't help it, she began yelling, her hands covering her body. She felt so violated.

"No. I swear. Melissa, Angel, look at me. I swear to you, I would never do that. I promised you I wouldn't and I never did. The only time I've ever gone into your mind was to bring you pleasure."

"Then how?" She was too angry to be embarrassed by his statement.

"Your nightmare. I was sleeping. I must have felt you struggling, in my arms, in your mind, I'm not sure exactly, but I know I shared your dream."

"No, that's impossible. Gareth showed me how to block my mind. How to block anyone from entering my dreams. He learned—got instructions from one of the best sorcerers in the country. There's no way you could have slid into my dream." She shook her head.

"Those methods work most of the time. But there are circumstances…"

Closing her eyes, Melissa couldn't bear to look at him when she asked the next question. "What did you see?" A tear slid down her cheek.

"Everything," he admitted softly. "Look at me, Mel."

She shook her head, refusing to see the pity in his face. *No wonder he hasn't wanted to be near me the past few nights.* A knife twisted in her heart as she realized how much he must pity her. *No wonder he wants to break up with me. Hell, after finding that information out, I'd want to break up with myself.*

"Just get it over with. Just break up with me now and get it over with. I don't need to look at you while you do that."

"Mel, Angel…I wish you could see yourself through my eyes. I—" Duncan grew quiet. She was tempted to open her eyes, to try to see what was going on inside his head. "I want you to see what I see. Open your mouth," he commanded gently. Another tear slid down her face as she obeyed without thought. "Suck."

A warm coppery taste covered her tongue, and her eyes flew open. Duncan watched her intently as she automatically swallowed the blood.

"That should be enough." He pulled his finger from her mouth and licked the puncture wound. "I'm going to enter your mind—but only to show you the door. I'll talk you through this, love. Close your eyes and open your mind, allow your thoughts to roam where they want."

Nodding, she obeyed his instructions.

Chapter Twelve

"I've never done this. If you've had enough of my blood, you should feel me enter. You should be able to sense me and hear me speak to you."

Melissa nodded again. Her face scrunched slightly when she felt something unfamiliar in her mind. The feeling wasn't unpleasant; the touch was light and radiated warmth.

Can you hear me?

She automatically answered him aloud. "Yes. It's low, like a whisper, but I hear you."

"I want you to search for me inside your mind."

"I'll try." Melissa concentrated on finding the source of warmth in her mind. After a few minutes she felt a caress to her cheek as his image appeared in front of her closed eyes. He was smiling.

"Good." *"Now, follow me. Imagine a door, see yourself following me through it. Don't be afraid if you don't recognize anything around you."* Duncan reached for her hand and Melissa was surprised when she felt it close around her own, even though part of her brain told her she could still feel both of his hands resting on her knees. *"I'll be beside you every step of the way. I won't let anything happen to you."*

She allowed him to lead her. Her breathing grew quicker when she felt herself moving in unfamiliar surroundings. Her first instinct was to pull away, to retreat as fast as she could back to everything familiar.

"*Don't fight it.*" Giving a gentle tug, he pulled her farther inside of his head. Opening his eyes, she gasped as she saw herself sitting in the chair. But instead of the image she'd seen reflected to her when she looked in the mirror as she dressed, she saw a woman who could be a model.

Her long hair looked like expensive silk, her skin was creamy and appeared flawless. Her lips were parted slightly and she felt the urge to kiss them. Arms circled her waist.

"*When I look at you, this is what I see. A beautiful woman. The most beautiful woman I've ever seen.*"

"*I don't really look like that.*"

"*Yes, you do. Angel, to me you are everything I could want. You don't have to take my word for it. Just look around. My thoughts, my feelings are here for you to see. Nothing is hidden.*"

Melissa swallowed the lump in her throat. "*I can look anywhere?*"

"*Anywhere.*"

Suddenly she was surrounded by doors. Opening the first one to her left, she was pushed back into his arms by the sudden overwhelming desire flooding her. Straightening, she stepped through the open door once again and saw herself in his arms. His thoughts drifted around her.

She's so beautiful. I don't deserve such an angel in my life. I don't even think she realizes exactly what she's given to me tonight.

Tears filled her eyes as she listened to his thoughts. They had just made love for the second time, and as she watched herself sleeping, she was astonished by the depth of his thoughts. Nowhere could she detect anything but utter contentment and concern as he wondered if he had hurt her. She felt his refusal to snoop inside her mind to gain an answer, to gain peace of mind.

Stepping out of the memory, she looked at the doors.

"*Duncan, you don't have to do this—*" she began.

"*I want you to know the truth. You deserve to know the truth about me before this goes any farther.*"

He led her down the hall. The longer they walked, the colder she felt, actually shivering from the lack of warmth.

"*Why is it so cold?*"

"*This is my past Melissa. This is the man I was, the man I am. This is the real me, the one you need to see.*" He gestured to the doors.

Looking around she didn't want to open any of the doors, but she knew she had to see one memory, if only to give him peace.

Opening a door on the right, she stepped through it alone.

ᘓᘔᘓ

Duncan looked at the woman wearing a once-stylish dress, her face haggard. Hair that used to gleam in the light surrounded her face, now limp and dull.

"I need more time," she pleaded.

He stood there, not giving her any clues to his thoughts.

"I'll do anything."

He considered her offer. It would be nothing to him to pay her debt off. She could clean his house; perhaps warm his bed once she got off the drugs poisoning her system. Even now he could see that she was pretty.

Duncan opened his mouth to accept her offer, but the woman pressed forward, trying to save herself.

"You can have my daughter for more time. Mary Louise," she yelled.

A girl came out from some back room wearing little more than rags, hugging the wall as she moved. It was clear she was afraid. She couldn't have been older than sixteen.

"She's a virgin. She'll let you do anything you want to her. I promise she won't fight you. If you give me more time, her virginity is yours." The girl flinched but stayed where she was, her head bowed as her mother tried to barter her body. "Show him," the mother ordered. The girl slowly lowered herself to her knees.

146

Fury consumed him. What mother would give her child to a man for more time? It was the wrong move. The girl's hands were on his pants as she began to unbutton them. Duncan quickly stepped back, not allowing her to go any farther, his anger growing when the girl flinched as he moved away from her.

"What good are you to me? You've been nothing but trouble since you were born. Now you can't even help me to gain a few more days to pay off my debt."

His eyes narrowed and his voice was as cold as ice when he spoke. "You are giving your daughter to me?"

The woman nodded enthusiastically.

"To treat however I please?"

"Of course. She is yours." Mary Louise flinched at her mother's rejection.

"Let's see how well she can obey commands. Mary Louise, close your eyes. Now," he commanded. She looked up at him, her eyes pleading, filled with terror. But he refused to respond, keeping his face carefully emotionless.

"You heard him," the mother screamed. She raised her hand threateningly and Mary Louise flinched. The girl's eyes closed instantly. "If she does not listen, slapping her or limiting how much she eats works well. Do these and I promise she will quickly learn to please you."

"Keep your eyes closed until I tell you otherwise." He waited until the girl signaled that she understood, her head bowed in subservience.

Silently he stepped around where Mary Louise still knelt on the hard wooden floor.

"Keep her for as long as she pleases you," the mother continued, unaware of his intentions. Before she could say another word that would hurt her daughter, his hand closed over her mouth.

"You will repeat what I tell you. Do you understand me?" he hissed in her ear, applying pressure to her flesh until the woman agreed. "Say Mary Louise, I love you." Duncan shifted his hand from her mouth to her throat.

"Mary Louise, I love you."

"Tell her you will miss her, and when she sees you again things will be different. And you better sound like you mean it. Tell her you're going to get help and things will be better," he hissed, applying more pressure to her throat.

Afraid for her life, the woman had tears in her eyes and his grip on her throat caused her voice to sound hoarse, as though she really meant what she was saying. "I'm going to miss you baby. I'm going to miss you so much. You be good for Mr. Stone, you do what he tells you. And Mary Louise, I'm going to get some help. I'm going to be different the next time you see me. Things will be better."

"Good," he whispered. "Now, go give her a hug and a kiss, and don't try anything stupid."

He watched, eyes still narrowed, as the woman knelt to give her daughter a hug and a kiss, cradling her daughter close.

"Mary Louise, are your eyes still closed?" Duncan asked when the mother released her.

"Yes sir," she responded, her voice low, emotion making her voice thick.

Gripping the woman's arm he pulled her into a back room. Disgust still filled him at the way she could give up her daughter so easily. He wanted to allow her to live long enough to regret how she had mistreated her daughter. Instead, he looked into her eyes.

The look on her face said she knew he was going to kill her. His thoughts returned to the girl still waiting for him on her knees. He decided to make it quick so Mary Louise wouldn't be left waiting much longer. Using his increased speed, he waited until she blinked. His hands moved so fast she didn't even have time to reopen her eyes as her neck snapped.

Allowing her body to fall soundlessly to the floor, Duncan left it as he reentered the room where Mary Louise awaited him.

Taking her elbow gently in his hand, he guided her up and out of the house.

"Thank you," she told him, her eyes still closed and her voice quiet as he helped her into the car awaiting him outside.

"For what?" Leaning forward, he gave the driver directions to their next destination.

"My mother has never told me she loved me a single day in my life. I know you had something to do with it."

He looked at her beside him in the back seat of the car. Despite her closed eyes, he could still see the tears that flowed down her cheeks.

"I'm never going to see her again, am I?"

He debated about lying to her for only a few seconds before deciding to be honest. "No."

"What are you going to do with me?"

In the darkness he could see her trembling. "I promise no harm will come to you."

Mary Louise sniffed. She didn't speak again during the remainder of their ride.

"I want you to stay here until I return."

"Yes sir," she answered, head still bowed. Climbing out of the car quickly, he walked purposefully up the path to the elegant front door. After knocking on it a few times, a man answered the door.

"What do you wan—" His face blanched white when he saw Duncan standing there.

"I'm collecting the debt you owe me. I have a girl in the car. You will invite her into your home. You will become her guardian and you will treat her as though she were a princess. Anything she wants, she gets. You will make sure she has a new wardrobe—only the best clothes and styles. Silks and velvets, nothing cheap. And most importantly, you will make certain no man ever hurts her or takes advantage of her."

"And…and if I fail?"

"Then you can expect another visit from me. And I promise, you will feel much pain."

Sandy Lynn

The man looked as though he were going to pass out.

"I understand. She'll be well taken care of."

"I know she will." Turning, Duncan returned to the car. Guiding Mary Louise to the awaiting man, he finally told her, "You may open your eyes. Mary Louise, this is Joseph. He will act as your guardian. If he ever mistreats you, I will know about it, and I will return to fix the problem." On impulse, he kissed the girl's forehead. "You should get some sleep. You will have a busy day tomorrow. Joseph will be taking you shopping for clothes and other necessities."

Returning to the car once the girl was safely inside the house, he instructed the driver to take him to another house nearby.

Within minutes he was standing in front of another, slightly more elegant door. This time a short, pudgy, balding man answered the door.

Without preamble he said, "I want to set up an account for a girl named Mary Louise."

CRBD

Duncan remained where he was, kneeling in front of her, watching closely as Melissa opened her eyes, and looked at him. What would she say about what she'd seen? Would she run from him as fast as she could? He wouldn't blame her if she did.

After several minutes of silence, he cleared his throat. "I'll walk you back down to the club. I won't bother you again."

"Duncan..."

"No, it's fine. I understand completely. I'm not the kind of man you deserve. I'm not a hero. In this life, I'm the villain."

"You saved that girl."

"And I killed her mother. Angel, I killed her; snapped her neck like it was a twig. I didn't hesitate. I didn't feel any guilt or regret. I still don't."

150

"You saved her daughter. You saved Mary Louise. You took her to a place where she would be safe, you made sure she could have anything she needed, she could possibly want. You aren't a monster, you saved her. Look at what her mother was going to do to her."

He should have known she would try to defend him even after what he'd shown her. "Angel..."

"No, don't you 'Angel' me. Yes, it was wrong of you to kill that woman. But you saved another life. What happened to her? What happened to Mary Louise?"

He closed his eyes, her image appearing. "She blossomed into a beautiful woman. She went to the best schools and married a man who swept her off her feet. He was the youngest son of a politician. If he could've, he'd have put a bow on the moon and handed it to her."

"She never saw you again." It wasn't a question.

"No. But I made sure she was kept safe. I made sure she never had to do without. Her wedding was one of the most elegant affairs of the year. She was denied nothing. Over half the city was invited. And everyone knew they better not start trouble that day or night. Word got out to all the bosses, all the leaders of every gang that if anyone so much as jaywalked the night she got married they would be seeing me—the one responsible for the action would be punished, and so would they for not controlling their people."

"A day without crime. The most perfect day you could give her. Not even her own father could have cared for her more."

Duncan shrugged. "I took her mom away. Besides, the bank manager handling my accounts was getting too fat."

"You gave her a new start. You gave her things she could only have dreamt of having. And I'm sure she never forgot you."

He shrugged again.

"Why are you so determined to make me see you as cruel and uncaring?"

"I just want you to know the truth, Mel. I don't want you to wake up a few months, or even a few years from now and regret staying with me. I don't

151

want you to feel like you settled and wonder how you could be with such a cold bastard."

She stared at him. "Are you asking…are you saying what I think you're saying? Gods, I have to be dreaming. Could you be a little more blunt please, cause I can't be understanding you right."

"Angel, I love being with you. I want to spend as much time with you as you will allow. I want—would you consider becoming a vampire? I couldn't stand the thought of losing you."

"And yes, love, as soon as I can get to a jewelers I will be asking exactly what you think I am."

Her face turned rosy. "I'm not sure I was supposed to hear that."

Smiling, Duncan lifted her out of the chair and sat down, placing her on his lap. He didn't respond to her comment. He pulled her close and placed a gentle kiss on her lips.

Melissa settled back against him. "So what do you do up here, while you're watching everyone?"

Maneuvering the chair backwards to lock the door, Duncan smiled when she blushed again. "I guess that depends."

"On?"

"On who is in the back room." He pointed to the monitors that showed the room was empty. "Or if I see anyone about to start shit on the dance floor." Today was the first time that he'd ever given less than his full attention to his job. If something happened when he hadn't been paying attention, he'd never forgive himself even though he was sure Bram would understand. This was important to him, and in all the years he'd worked at Club Strigoi, he was one of the very few bouncers who paid attention to his job instead of goofing off. Even if he did jerk off occasionally.

"How can you tell?"

"I can't always, but there are little signs I look for. A woman that doesn't want to dance with a guy will nudge him away from her. She'll move his hands off her body or reposition them. Sometimes she'll try to step away."

"How can you see the signs when the floor gets so crowded?"

"It's not easy, but, it's not hard to notice the two that look like they are fighting among a crowded floor where everyone is happily moving with the music."

Duncan smiled, waiting for the question he knew was coming without peaking inside her mind.

"How many times have you watched me on those monitors?"

"Since we've been together? Every night you've been here." He nipped her neck and she squirmed deliciously on his lap.

"How—"

"Shhhh. I won't do anything you don't want me to do."

She leaned back against him, her body relaxing, questions stopping. Pulling her shirt loose from the jeans she always wore, he removed her shirt. His hand moved against her bare skin until he was cupping her breast.

Melissa gave a low moan as he tweaked her nipple through the lace of her bra. Easing his hands up her chest to her shoulder, he gently slid the straps off her shoulders before unclasping her bra. As she watched, the lacy garment fell to the floor beside her. Lifting her off his lap, his hands went to her jeans, unbuttoning them and sliding them down her hips.

"Who—wait. That's Heath."

She leaned forward, presenting Duncan with a view of her ass, clad only in bikini style underwear that made his mouth water.

"I haven't seen him around in…" She paused. "I don't even remember. I'm a bad friend. What if he'd been hurt? What if he needed help?"

"Angel, you can't be everywhere." His hands slid up her bare thighs, his hunger growing. He wanted all of her, couldn't get enough. As surely as some people were addicted to drugs or alcohol, he had eagerly fallen into his own addiction. Melissa.

"Is there a way to cut the monitors off? We shouldn't spy on them."

"No. You'd be surprised how many times we've had to stop something back there. Make out sessions gone bad where the lady would have been raped if someone hadn't been watching." Looking around her perfect ass, Duncan glanced at the screen. The couple was sitting on the ratty green couch. He smiled. No matter how shitty it looked, it was the most comfortable couch he'd ever sat on.

Glancing up at her face, he saw disbelief as she watched the screen. His gaze returned to the screen, it was becoming apparent what the couple was back there to do. Duncan's hands stroked up and down Melissa's thighs as she stood, mesmerized by what she was watching.

With gentle movements he parted her legs, his fingers moving effortlessly over the satin covering her sex. Feeling the moisture soaking into the material he leaned closer, nibbling on her ass. A gasp escaped her.

We shouldn't watch them," she said, unable to look away.

Instead of answering, Duncan continued to tease her with his mouth. Her eyes drifted shut as she concentrated on what he was doing. Inside her mind she tried to find the door he'd guided her through. Opening it timidly, she was surprised at the warmth that seemed to fill her body. All over, her skin tingled as though Duncan had suddenly developed six more hands.

"Are you sure?" he asked behind her, before his tongue smoothed over the bottom of her ass.

"Yes," she sent back. Within seconds she felt him inside her mind, felt him standing behind her, his hard cock pressing against her ass even as she felt his tongue tracing patterns on her flesh.

"Watch the screen," the Duncan in her mind whispered in her ear. In her mind, both of his hands cupped her breasts, pinching her nipples lightly. In the surveillance room, she felt him pull her panties down.

The sensations were so real—both of them—she was quickly losing track of which was real and which were in her mind. It was as though she had two men catering to her every need, worshiping every inch of her body.

His fingers slid inside her dripping pussy as his tongue stroked her ear.

"Too much," she moaned inside her head, still watching the screen where Heath and some blonde were now having sex on the old couch. She was on top of his lap, riding him with her head thrown back.

154

She ached to feel Duncan thrusting inside of her. That image only added to the images filling her mind, heightening her desire.

Duncan stood up behind her, parting her legs more then pushed deep inside of her.

"Gods you're so wet," he moaned as the other Duncan circled to stand in front of her. Melissa's eyes closed as she wrapped her arms around his neck pulling him down into a hungry kiss. Fingers began to play with her clit as hands held her close, wrapping in her hair.

"Gods," she cried out. She wasn't even sure if she was screaming aloud or inside her mind, and it wasn't important. Teeth grazed the back of her neck, as the form she was kissing pulled away. Kissing his way down her body, he knelt between her legs. After a second of looking up at her like that, he leaned into her body, his tongue stroking her folds as the cock slid in and out of her pussy.

"Love..." one of the forms groaned, creating an echo.

"Yes, Duncan, do it."

As teeth slid into her flesh, her entire body exploded. The force of her orgasm ripped through her body, her mind, her heart and her soul. In her mind she saw an explosion of color that would rival any fireworks display she'd ever seen. Every part of her trembled from the aftershocks as Duncan growled. She felt his tongue gliding over her flesh, closing the wound seconds before he stopped moving. The kneeling Duncan caught her as she fell to the floor, her limbs unable to support her any longer. Behind her, arms wrapped around her waist and pulled her backward until she was sitting on his lap. Cracking her eyes open, she could see the monitors in front of her.

Her head fell back against him. Both Duncans kissed opposite sides of her neck as they held her close.

Her heartbeat was hard inside of her chest. "What did you do to me?" She heard an echo of her words in her head.

His chest vibrated beneath her.

"How could you do that? How is it possible?"

"It's not easy. Did you enjoy it?"

"Gods, yes," she moaned.

"I'm glad." He kissed her neck again. "Get some rest, Angel."

"What about you?" she asked sleepily.

"As long as you're in my arms I'll be just fine."

As much as she hated admitting it, Melissa wasn't sure she'd be able to keep her eyes open. Her body felt so relaxed, she felt so…satisfied. A smile curved her lips.

Her head was turned to the side and a gentle kiss placed on her lips. "I'm glad Angel. And we are going to have to work on your shields." He chuckled before she felt him pulling away, leaving her mind.

Inside her mind she felt a chill as his warmth began to fade. "Don't. Not yet. Please, hold me. Both of you hold me?"

He nodded and she felt two sets of arms cradling her close to the man—men?—she loved as she drifted to sleep.

Chapter Thirteen

Melissa stretched in the soft bed. She felt as though she were lying on a cloud. She felt so warm and safe. Propping herself up she glanced around Duncan's bedroom.

As though her thoughts conjured him, he appeared through the door. "Hungry?"

"Starving." She smiled as she sat up, allowing the blankets to puddle in her lap. Watching him, she enjoyed seeing the hungry look that came into his eyes whenever he saw her body. In his bedroom, it had been easy to release her fears. She couldn't remember wearing clothes at all in the few nights and days she'd been there.

Looking at him, she sighed contentedly. "I want to introduce you to my brother," she blurted out.

"We've met," he chuckled. "I know all of the regulars."

"Yeah, but he hasn't been introduced to you as my boyfriend."

"When would you like to do that?"

"Tonight? If you're going to change me, I—I want his blessing, Duncan. Gods that makes me sound like some little girl doesn't it?"

"Not at all. I'd be more surprised if you didn't want it. But I think we should take you shopping first. I'm pretty sure he wouldn't like to see you appear wearing rags."

"My clothes…" She blushed as she remembered the rush they had been in to remove her clothing when they arrived at his room. How she'd growled that she didn't care how rough he was so long as he was buried inside of her as quickly as possible.

"Got a little torn when we got to my room," he finished for her.

Melissa chuckled. They had both been in a hurry to get her out of them when they reached the bed.

"Okay, then how about this. I'll jump into the shower and call Gareth after I get out. I'll steal a shirt from you then we can go buy me a new outfit to wear after breakfast. I'll change before we speak with my brother."

"Sounds like a plan. Don't take too long in the shower, or we might have to postpone your plans." He got a twinkle in his eyes. "I might not be able to help myself if I have to come in and get you."

Standing, she headed for the small bathroom connected to his room. When she looked back, she smiled mischievously and blew him a kiss before making her way to the shower. Beneath the hot water she was amazed at how wonderful her life was. It was almost as though nothing could go wrong.

Wrapped in a towel she reentered the bedroom quietly, watching Duncan pull jeans over his hips as he spoke on the phone.

"Tomorrow night, gotcha. Thank you for getting back to me on this." He paused. "Okay, I'll see you then." He hung up the phone.

"What was that about?" Melissa asked as she pulled on first her underwear then her tattered jeans.

"Oh, I called a piercer friend of mine a few weeks ago. He just returned the call."

"A few weeks ago? Why so long to get back to you?"

"Well, first he was on vacation, and you can't blame a man for wanting to take his beautiful girlfriend to a beach so he can ogle her in a bikini." As he spoke he walked closer to her, nipping her neck lightly when he pulled her into his arms.

"I have to get dressed," she protested weakly.

"But I like you better naked."

"I don't think my brother would appreciate that," she teased.

"Good point." He stepped back to watch her pull her bra on, continuing with their conversation. "Then when he got back from vacation, he had to go to a convention. He's just getting back to town, so…" He shrugged.

"So, what are you getting pierced? Can I grab a shirt?"

He nodded to the closet. "Help yourself. Maybe I shouldn't tell you, and just let it be a surprise."

"That would be cruel. If you don't tell me I'll be wondering about it all night. How can I hold a conversation like that?" Going through his closet she pulled out a basic black shirt and quickly slipped into it. His scent surrounded her. Even though she was dressed, she continued to look through his clothes. When she saw a dark blue shirt with a wolf on the front she pulled it out and tossed it to him.

"Hmmm, would that get me out of talking with your brother?"

"No. It would just leave me too distracted to defend you." Melissa walked over to him and straddled his lap before kissing him deeply.

"Well, when you put it that way…" His arms wrapped around her, pressing her closer to him. As they kissed again, Duncan leaned back until she was sprawled on top of him. His hand dove beneath the shirt she wore to caress her breast.

"No fair."

"Fair is overrated."

"Tell me?" She pressed kisses to his face then bit down on his ear.

"I'm getting a ladder."

"A ladder?"

"Jacob's Ladder."

"What's that?"

His eyes sparkled with mischief as his hips lifted both of them from the bed. Somehow he managed to pull his pants down. His cock, freed from its confines, reached for her. Taking her hand in his, he rubbed it against the smooth underside of his dick. "Barbells, spaced apart, here."

"Won't that hurt? Why would you want to do that? You know you're a freak, right?" Her hand continued to stroke him lightly.

"I've wanted it for a little while. And it's supposed to increase her pleasure."

"By her, you mean me right?" she teased.

"Of course. If you don't like it, I'll take 'em out. But I am getting them, Mel."

"I trust you, Duncan. I don't think I'd deny you much. You're *my* freak and I love you."

"Much? Angel, if you keep doing that, we are not meeting with your brother tonight."

She gave one last stroke before climbing off of him. "Well, I don't think I could ever share you with another woman. So, I can't say I would deny you nothing…"

"Call your brother, Angel. I'm not sure how much longer I can control myself if we stay in here with such an inviting bed."

Laughing, she dialed her brother's cell phone.

CB⊗

Duncan sighed. Melissa had him wrapped around her little finger, and to be honest, he wasn't sure that he truly minded. He was not looking forward to Gareth's expression when he discovered just who his little sister was dating, though. Too soon, they arrived at Lalita's apartment.

Looking down at the woman he'd fallen so helplessly in love with, he smiled as he stared at her. She'd bought a pair of snug, dark-blue jeans that hugged her ass. The tantalizing black top she wore showed off the marks he'd left on her neck and chest.

Watching Melissa, Duncan knew he'd be buying her a ring the next night, after he finished meeting with Jake. But right now he wanted to take her back to his place and pull her clothes off, showing her a good old-fashioned ravishing.

Before he could make the suggestion, she reached out and knocked on the door and he sent a prayer of thanks it was La who answered the door. To his surprise, she was dressed much like Melissa.

"I did *not* see that coming," she said, laughter filling her voice. "Oh this is gonna be rich. Damn, is there enough time for me to get my video camera?"

"La," Melissa scolded.

"Come on in you two. Gareth should be back in a couple of minutes. He just had to run to the store."

Duncan followed Melissa into the apartment. Looking around at the floral patterns, he was shocked at the décor. It looked so different from what he expected—not that he'd put much thought into what Lalita's home would look like, but this was almost the exact opposite of what he would have imagined if he had.

"You have a lovely home."

"Yeah, yeah, thank my sister," she mumbled. "Why don't you two have a seat and I'll go hide the knives."

"Why?"

"You didn't tell her?" La asked Duncan, shocked.

He shrugged.

"Mel, honey, everyone knows..." Lalita's statement was ended when the door opened.

"La, they didn't have the big packs, so I just grabbed a couple of the smaller boxes. That should get us through—You."

The bag Gareth was carrying dropped from his hand and Duncan had just enough time to get away from Melissa so she wouldn't get hurt accidentally before Gareth tried to tackle him.

Moving away from the couch, he dodged the other man's punches.

"I'm gonna kill you. Who the fuck do you think you are? How dare you touch my sister!"

"Stop," Melissa screamed, distracting Duncan long enough that one of Gareth's blows landed across his jaw.

Growling, he pushed the other man away, not wanting to hurt the brother of the woman he loved. But that didn't stop Gareth. It was clear Gareth wanted to spill Duncan's blood. Baring his fangs, Gareth rushed at Duncan, and managed to back him into a corner.

"I don't want to hurt you," Duncan told him through clenched teeth.

"Too bad, cause I really don't have a problem beating the shit out of you."

"Gareth, don't you dare punch a hole in my wall. Do you know how irritating it is to have to call a repairman then have to get the whole place soundproofed again?"

"Gareth, stop," Melissa pleaded.

Duncan glanced over to her, shocked to see the fear in her eyes. *"Don't worry Angel, he isn't going to hurt me. And I promise, no matter how much I want to, I won't hurt him...too badly."*

He saw her nod slightly, just before he felt her brother's hands around his neck.

"Don't. Make. Me. Hurt you," Duncan said as the other man squeezed his throat as hard as he could.

"Leave my sister alone. I don't want to even hear that you were in the same room with her ever again, you bastard."

"That's up to her. I'll ask you one more time, to let go of me. Don't make me hurt you."

Gareth laughed. Using the skills he'd perfected a century ago, Duncan applied pressure to the other man's inner arm, careful not to do any permanent damage even as black spots began to appear in front of him. The man's grip loosened and he pressed his advantage. Within seconds, he had

Gareth's arm pinned behind his back with enough pressure that the slightest amount of additional pressure would break the bone in half.

Pushing the man away from him, his eyes narrowed as he resisted the urge to rub the sore muscles of his throat.

Why the fuck does everyone have to go for my neck?

Gareth growled and looked as though he wanted to leap for him again, but Melissa quickly stood between the two men. Walking backwards, she continued until her back pressed against Duncan's body. His discomfort was forgotten as his arms circled her waist.

"Don't," she said to her brother. Turning in his arms, Melissa ran her hands over the bruises he was sure had appeared on his flesh. "Gods, Duncan, I'm so sorry. If I'd have known what an asshole my brother was going to be I'd have never asked you to come tonight."

"Don't worry about it, Angel. He's just trying to protect you. I can't blame him for that."

"I can." Turning again, she rested her head back against his chest. "I love him, Gareth."

"You can't love him. He's a...he cannot be the man you told me about. Mel, he doesn't stay with a woman. He gets what he wants then he's out of there faster than you can ask 'where are you going?' I won't let him hurt you like that."

"If he's so intent on hurting me, why did he come here to meet you? Gareth if he only wanted to fuck me and leave, why didn't he leave me weeks ago?" she shouted.

Gareth's face paled, and Lalita came up behind him.

"That's enough. Why don't we all just sit down and talk about this like adults?"

Duncan nodded and, taking Melissa's hand in his own, he led her over to the couch then sat down in one of the chairs.

"Gareth, I love him."

Sandy Lynn

"He's going to hurt you," he told her softly, leaning back against Lalita as she tried to soothe him.

"No he's not. I love him. I trust him. Gareth, Duncan's going to change me." She looked back at him shyly.

Gareth looked as though she'd just told him she was going to stake him.

Duncan had to give the other man credit. Even though he looked as though he'd rather be slowly poisoned and suffer a painful death, he was polite. "If you hurt my sister I will kill you."

"If I hurt her, I'd deserve to die."

⋐✠⋑

Travis was growing impatient as he stood across the street from the unimpressive building. After weeks of watching and waiting, always so close to his revenge but unable to take it, he was growing annoyed. Did they always have to travel around in groups?

He knew he should have grabbed that vampire bastard before he'd entered the brick building. But no, he'd hesitated just a second too long. Hatred filled him. Even after twelve years, Travis could still feel the creature's teeth slipping into his flesh, the way his lips suckled on his neck. A shudder went down his body. He'd always heard vampires didn't touch members of the same sex—just look at all those Hollywood movies—but he knew different. It didn't matter what gender you were, so long as your blood was warm.

Looking at that bastard, being so close to him, brought back the memory of laughter. He'd been laughed at when he entered the bar, holding his neck, with no wound visible. That had surprised him. He'd been stunned when he finally looked into a mirror and couldn't see any sign of the unholy kiss he'd received. It humiliated him.

He could still remember the way the creature flashed his fangs as he came to take Melissa away. He hadn't said a word, but the threat was clear.

Pacing in the shadows, he allowed his anger, his hatred to strengthen his resolve. Justice would be his. He just needed to be a little more patient.

164

08⁊0

Duncan looked around the club, it just wasn't the same without Melissa. Somehow she'd managed to turn his life around completely. He wanted to be a better man for her.

He had managed to convince her to spend the night shopping with Mona. He knew he'd need at least the one night for his body to adjust to the piercings, and after he met with Jake, he'd scheduled a meeting with a jeweler to see their selection. If she were at CS, he wouldn't be able to think about anything other than getting her back up to his room.

Jake entered and Duncan walked over to meet him. Directing the piercer to the back room, Duncan gave him a few minutes to unpack his bag before he followed. He went to the bar and got a glass of water. When it was finished, he placed the glass back on the bar. Tonight would be hell, he already wanted Melissa in his arms, but he wouldn't get to see her again until the following night.

Duncan strolled across the dance floor, his brow creasing slightly when he saw Lalita and Bram talking. Shrugging, he figured it wasn't any of his business and entered the room.

"So, what are you getting?" Jake asked.

"I want a Jacob's Ladder."

Jake nodded. "Frenum Ladder," he said, giving the technical name for the piercing. "Gotcha. How many bars?"

"Four for now." Dropping his pants, Duncan lay down on the table, waiting for the process to begin. At first it felt weird to feel another man's hands wrapped around his cock, but this was something he knew he wanted.

"How far apart do you want them?" Jake asked after the first marks were centered.

"About three-eighths of an inch apart." After a few minutes he felt the needle slide through his flesh, quickly replaced by cold metal. The sensation was repeated three more times as he lay on the table thinking about Melissa.

165

"Okay, you're all set. You really don't want to irritate it tonight. I probably should go into my usual aftercare speech, but I don't know how much of it applies to vampires. But you definitely don't want to irritate it tonight."

Duncan laughed. "I know. That's why I told my girl I couldn't see her tonight. What do I owe you?"

"No charge. Dude, I owe you much more than a few minutes of my time. Shit, man, if not for you—"

"That's all in the past. What do I owe you?"

"Nothing. I won't take money from you. Now, to the aftercare. Because of your accelerated healing, you'll probably be fine tomorrow night—but I'd recommend at least using condoms, and extra lube—for the next few nights. If you take them out, you'll probably have to get repierced, unless you're replacing the jewelry immediately. Rinse them well with water, you want to keep those things clean to prevent any irritation. Go easy on the soap, especially tonight, since that can dry your skin out. And trust me, you're going to want to wear loose jeans."

"I'll keep that in mind." Duncan chuckled as he pulled up his pants, making sure they rested low on his hips, giving his groin as much room as possible.

"So, you've got a girl now?"

Duncan smiled. "Mel. I don't know what I did right in this life to deserve her, cause fuck if I can think of anything."

"You've done a lot of good. You've saved a lot of lives, mine included."

"And I've done a hell of a lot more evil. Why do you people defend me?"

"Ah, Mel won't let you call yourself evil either huh? I like her already. We won't let you do it because you're a good guy. Whatever you were in your past, that's not who you are now."

"You're wrong. That's exactly who I still am. I didn't want to ask this on the phone, but I need to know if you've heard of a man named Travis Long hanging around town."

Jake shook his head. "Doesn't sound familiar. But then, I am just getting back in town. You want me to ask a couple of guys?"

"I'd appreciate it."

"I'll make a few calls as soon as I'm done here."

"Thanks man." Duncan shook the other man's hand. "And if you ever need anything, you know you can call me."

"I know."

As Duncan left the room, he tugged on his jeans and smiled when he saw Bram standing outside the door. Exiting the club, humming as he went, he headed for the jewelers down the street. The sign on the door said closed, but as soon as he knocked, the owner's face appeared and he motioned for Duncan to go around the side of the building.

"I appreciate you staying late for me. I had a previous appointment."

"No problem, Mr. Stone. My manager told me that you are looking to buy a ring. We have quite a nice selection. What kind were you looking to buy exactly?"

"Something special. I want an engagement ring, but not the type of thing you would see everywhere."

"Were you looking for something in particular?"

Duncan shook his head. "I'll know it when I see it."

Three hours and countless rings later, he was ready to give up on ever finding anything that would be perfect, especially since he'd gone through the man's entire stock, and not just of engagement rings.

"There's only one ring left that you haven't seen, Mr. Stone. It just arrived today." The man went into the back of the shop and returned with a small velvet box. Opening the box, Duncan stared at the perfect ring.

"An emerald cut black diamond, surrounded by smaller clear diamonds. Total carat weight is—"

"I don't care."

"Mr. Stone…"

"I don't care. I want this ring. Now," he pulled out his wallet and fanned out his credit cards, "pick a card and wrap it up." Typically he would never be so blatant about how much money he had, but he was not in the mood to hear the owner of the store tell him how expensive or whatever the ring was. It was perfect and that was all that mattered.

Chapter Fourteen

Melissa looked in the mirror. She looked so different. On the phone, Duncan had told her he had a surprise for her tonight, and he didn't mean the piercing. She felt giddy. Was tonight the night he'd propose? The night he'd change her? Whatever it was, she wanted to look special. She wasn't sure why she'd allowed Mona to talk her into buying the slinky black dress the previous night, but now she was thankful the woman had insisted.

Standing in the bathroom, she even spent extra time on her hair, pulling out her hated curling iron and twisting the long strands into something that looked elegant. She didn't care if his surprise was Duncan simply telling her he loved her, she wanted to look special for him tonight.

He'd never know precisely how much he meant to her. She paused, her hand freezing before she could apply the eye shadow. *Well, he could know if he looked.* Closing her eyes, she searched for him. She still wasn't very good at the telepathic communications, but she could feel the warmth radiating from the door that would lead her to Duncan. It was always there with her now that she'd tasted his blood. That thought more than any other managed to bring her peace.

Smiling at her reflection, she sighed happily. There really wasn't anything to worry about. Her stepfather couldn't or wouldn't touch her. She was surrounded by wonderful friends, and people who loved her—even if one of them hadn't exactly said it yet.

It doesn't matter. He wouldn't change me if he didn't love me. He shows me he loves me in everything he does, the way he holds me. He can tell me when he's ready.

Sandy Lynn

The thought brought no bitterness. Being inside his mind, seeing what he saw, she felt the happiness that surrounded him when she was near. Stepping away from the counter, she put on her low heels and carefully walked downstairs.

As she passed the kitchen, the phone rang. "Hello?"

"Hey Mel. Are we gonna see you at CS tonight or do you and…do you have plans?"

"Gareth, I'm on my way to the club now. I think you'll be shocked when you see me."

"Why, did you finally cover the hickeys?" her brother grumbled.

"Gareth!" She heard Lalita yell in the background. "I'm telling you this minute if you don't shut the fuck up and be happy for your sister, you can just go back to sleeping in your own bedroom. And no, I won't be there."

She couldn't help chuckling at her friend's threat. They were absolutely perfect together.

"Fine. La says I have to play nice. You'll stay long enough for me to see you? Maybe even let me dance with my baby sister?"

"It's a date. Just because Duncan and I are together doesn't mean I won't be your little sister. It doesn't mean that I won't have time to spend with you anymore."

"I know. I just… Dammit, I feel guilty, okay. If I hadn't let myself get so wrapped up in La, I'd have known what was going on. Maybe I'd have been able to do something…"

"I love you, Gareth. I'll see you in a little bit, my cab should be here any minute."

"Okay. Love you too, Mel. Always."

She hung up the phone. She knew her brother was just worried about her. That he only wanted to keep her safe. Grabbing her keys she walked out the front door, her head held high. A cab sat, waiting on the street in front of her house. Before she could lock the door, Melissa paused. Her smile faltered as the small hairs on the back of her neck stood up. Straightening slightly, she

170

began to turn around when a cloth covered her nose and mouth. She tried to struggle, to fight off her attacker.

"Didn't think you'd be safe from me forever, did you, you little bitch?"

She began to struggle harder against the man holding her, terrified of what would happen if she lost consciousness.

"Your freak of a protector couldn't watch you all the time. And look, you even dressed up for me."

Her struggles began to weaken as her limbs grew heavier.

Must stay awake, she told herself, but her thoughts were sluggish, as though she'd gone on some kind of alcohol binge.

Everything began to grow black, and she felt Travis's hand slide over her body in a way that would have had her retching if she weren't losing consciousness.

Mustering all the strength she had, she closed her eyes and stumbled through her mind. She couldn't even see where anything was, her brain was too fuzzy from the effects of the chemicals. But she knew she had only one chance to choose the right door.

Falling to the ground, she crawled the last few paces to a door that radiated warmth and happiness, praying it led to Duncan and not a memory of her mother. Opening the door, she just managed to scream out his name before she was sucked into the dark oblivion of unconsciousness.

CB♥SO

He was tired of waiting. He would have grabbed her the night before but she was with this weird bitch. Anytime he'd gotten close enough to her, his skin began to crawl. No doubt she was one of those freaky unnatural creatures as well. Probably a werewolf or siren or something. He'd seen her move around in the daylight, that was when their shopping trip had begun, so he was certain she wasn't a bloodsucker.

Travis's lip curled as he looked down at the unconscious woman in his lap. Soon. With any luck she and her "brother" had that link—the one he swore would let him find Travis wherever he went. But he'd learned just how much bullshit that was. How close had he been to them? How long had he been watching and waiting for the perfect opportunity to strike and never once been detected?

Now he would just have to bide his time until his revenge could be perfect—just the way he'd always planned it would be.

CℬℬƆ

Duncan was going through his closet, trying to decide what to wear. He wanted the night to be special for Melissa and not ruin it because he'd just thrown something on. Women were always going on about how they remembered the exact details of any special occasion, and he'd seen his share of disgusted looks when the memory included a less than perfectly dressed suitor.

Feeling the pocket of his jeans for what had to have been the sixth time, he felt the small box waiting to be pulled out and given to his angel.

When he heard the desperate scream inside his head, a chill went down his spine, making him feel as though he'd been plunged into an icy cold tub.

"Duncan!"

Automatically he began to run for her, to catch her through their connection, but when he tried to go through the door, it was like slamming into a brick wall.

"Mother fucker, son of a bitch." He screamed in frustration, grabbing the first thing he could put his hand on and throwing it across the room as hard as he could.

This is really bad. Beating his fists against the wall blocking him from his love, he'd never felt more helpless. The only way he knew to block a path so effectively was if she'd been knocked unconscious. Had she fallen and hurt herself? No, there was too much terror in her voice for that.

Someone must have hurt her. His head cleared as his anger began to simmer inside. Anyone from his past would know that's when he became truly dangerous.

Reaching for the phone to call her brother—as much as he didn't want to—he cursed under his breath as he saw the handset across the room, smashed into hundreds of pieces. Taking another deep breath, he grabbed a shirt from his closet and exhaled slowly as he pulled it on. He would just go downstairs to the club and use their phone.

Concentrating on his breathing, Duncan made his way down the stairs. At the bar he picked up the phone and quickly dialed Lalita's number.

When Gareth answered the phone, Duncan got straight to the point. "Have you spoken to Mel recently?"

"About ten minutes ago, why?"

"Nothing. I just got this strange feeling," Duncan lied easily. There was no sense in worrying her brother if this turned out to be nothing. "Probably just my nerves."

"Why would you be nervous? Planning on ruining her life?"

"No." He hung up the phone and began to dial Jake's number.

"What are you doing?" the blonde bartender asked curiously, walking over to him.

Glaring at her, Duncan growled, his eyes narrowed as he finished dialing the number. She moved to the other end of the bar.

Jake answered the phone and Duncan forced himself not to growl at the man. "I need you. Meet me at Club Strigoi in ten minutes." Without waiting for a response, he hung up the phone.

He strode purposefully to the door, and asked the guard, "Has a bleached blonde by the name of Diane been here lately?"

The man looked at him like he was crazy. As part of his mind continued to beat on the brick wall, determined to know the second she regained consciousness, he snapped. Picking the hefty man up as though he weighed no more than a small child, Duncan slammed him into the wall. "Have you seen a bleached blonde that goes by the name Diane come to the club lately?" He spoke slowly, carefully enunciating his words.

"I don't know who you're talking about. Do you know how many people I see come and go every night?"

"You'd recognize her. She's the bitch that was hitting on Gareth a few weeks ago."

"No. No, she hasn't been by in a couple of nights. I haven't seen her," the man told him, his voice whining.

Hands tugged on Duncan, trying to get him to release his grip on the other man.

"Duncan, man, calm down. Put the man down and we'll go find her," Jake promised.

Duncan released the bouncer, allowing him to fall into a heap to the floor. Striding out of the club, Duncan climbed into the beaten up truck that Jake drove.

"Who are we looking for?"

"A bleached blonde. Goes by the name of Diane."

"I'll make a few calls."

Jake began to drive, making phone calls as Duncan sat in the truck, looking out the window. He didn't know how long he'd been beating on the wall inside his head, but his hands felt bruised from the effort. They could crack and bleed for all he cared, he wouldn't give up.

"Can you give me anything else to go on? Those two details aren't much help."

"All I know is that she showed up at the club a month or so ago, and began hitting on one of the regulars."

"Damn. It'd be easier to find a needle in a haystack."

"I'm going to find her, Jake," he told the man, his voice lacking any emotion.

"What did she do to you? Cause the way you look man, this woman's gonna be lucky if you don't rip her apart, limb by limb."

"Yes. She will." He looked out the window. "Stop the car."

The man immediately pulled to the side, but Duncan was out of the car before it stopped. Door left wide open, he advanced on the blonde and catching her by the throat, forced her against the side of a building. "Where is he?"

"I don't know who you're talking about. Get this freak offa me," she yelled at Jake.

"Are you sure she's the one."

"It's her. Where is he? You are going to tell me where I can find Travis or I'm going to make your life very unpleasant. The whole thirty minutes you have left."

She opened her mouth to scream, and he added more pressure to her throat until she was gasping for air. Diane scratched at him, her hands trying to loosen his grip, her nails digging into his flesh, but he never looked away. Easing the pressure slightly, he spoke, his voice devoid of any emotion. "Where is Travis Long?"

"I don't know. I swear I don't. He contacted me. He gave me one of those prepaid cell phones and he called me. The last time I heard from him he said he didn't need my help anymore. I swear, it's the truth."

"Do you have a number on the phone?"

"He...he always used a-a payphone," she gasped.

Duncan released her. When she straightened, Diane's hands were around her neck and her breathing was hard. He could smell fear dripping from every pore. "If you are lying to me, there is nowhere you can run that will be far enough."

"I'm not lying. I swear," she repeated, her eyes wide and voice already growing hoarse from nearly being strangled.

"I hope for your sake you aren't," Jake said behind him as Duncan went back to the truck. "Do you remember anything? Trust me you don't want to be on my friend's bad side." A few seconds later, he joined Duncan in the truck. "I'll make a few more calls."

Sandy Lynn

The vehicle remained parked as Jake spoke on the phone. With a sigh, he hung up the phone. "None of my sources know anything, Duncan. Man, I'm sorry. What did this man do to make you want his blood so badly?"

"He hurt the woman I love." Looking at his friend he said, "Your sources can't find anything. It's time for me to collect on a few favors."

Nodding, Jake started the engine. As they began to drive, he said, "Give it an hour, hour and a half tops, you'll find him."

"I just hope Mel has an hour and a half."

ॐ

The first thing Melissa became aware of as she struggled to wake was the large wad of cotton in her mouth, sucking up any moisture. She moved her tongue to dislodge it, and was surprised to discover her mouth was empty. As she woke, her head felt like someone had been using it for target practice.

She wanted to sit up, to try to remember what had happened. Why was she lying down? She was supposed to meet Duncan at the club. He had a surprise for her.

A flood of warmth rushed into her mind. *"Don't move, Angel. No matter what, don't move. Don't speak, don't move; concentrate on keeping your breathing perfectly even."*

"What's going on?" She tried to press him for answers when Duncan took her into his arms. *"I don't remember anything after I spoke to Gareth. Oh gods,"* she panicked. *"Is he okay?"*

"Your brother is fine, Angel. Remember what I said. Stay as still as you can. Concentrate. What happened after you hung up the phone?"

Melissa fought to listen to him. He sounded so worried. What could have happened? *"I got my keys,"* she began slowly, the images becoming slightly less fuzzy. She moved in the bed slightly. *"It's hard. It's so hard to try to keep my mind and body separate."*

176

"*I know, Angel, I know.*" He caressed her hair. "*Please, try for me? I wouldn't ask if it wasn't important.*"

"*What's going on, Duncan? Am I hurt? Am I in the hospital?*"

"*What happened next?*"

"*I left the house. I remember getting this strange feeling, like someone was watching me…*" Her flesh began to crawl and her muscles jerked as the rest of her memory returned. She began to struggle, both in her mind and in the bed until Duncan wrapped his arms around her so tightly that she couldn't move. Feeling his steel grip on her, her body grew still, as though it too were pinned to the bed.

"*Oh gods, he's found me. He's got me Duncan, he's got me,*" she sobbed. "*Please tell me Gareth doesn't know. It's a trap. Travis is going to use me to kill my brother.*"

"*No, he won't.*"

"*Yes he will. You don't know him, he's evil.*"

"*Angel, listen to me,*" he told her gently, pressing a kiss to her forehead. "*That's why it's so important for you to remain calm. As long as he believes you're unconscious, you're safe. He's going to want to make sure you are alert before he does anything.*"

She nodded in her mind. "*I'll try.*"

"*No, love, you will. This is one time that try isn't good enough. I'm going to find you.*"

"*No,*" she screamed. "*I don't want you to see. Duncan, I don't want you to see me after he's—*"

He's not going to touch you. I promise, Angel, I promise.

৩৪০

Travis smiled as he hid in the shadows and watched her struggle to remain still. He'd allow her to play her game for now. He'd noticed how she jumped, her delicious struggles. He'd also caught the way her body jerked, as though she were being held still. No doubt she was in touch with someone.

Sandy Lynn

It had been a stroke of genius to knock her unconscious before he brought her home. If he hadn't, he may have had to bruise all that beautiful flesh as he tied her to the bed. As tempting as it had been, he'd managed to keep his hands off of her. But that hadn't stopped him from looking. First thing she would learn is that she needed to shave her pussy. He wanted her smooth, just the way she would've been all those years ago.

Besides, what fun would it be, punishing her without his intended audience? No, he'd allow her to send her pimp instructions, the few details she could give him.

He just hoped that she told him enough to help him get there quickly. His dick was already straining inside his jeans at the thought of enjoying her as she remained tied to the bed. She would remain tied to the bed during their fucking until she'd learned to love what he did to her.

No doubt that wouldn't take very long. She would surely be thankful he'd rescued her from those things that took pleasure out of draining her blood as they fucked her.

He'd also taken a good long look at the pucker of her ass. He wondered how many men had been there. He couldn't wait to bury himself inside of her. But again, he would be careful, making certain that she was unconscious before he flipped her around on the bed and retied her with her ass up.

More and more lustful thoughts entered his head of how he would use her body, how he would make her scream. Rubbing his hand over his jean-covered erection, Travis wondered if he would be able to wait until their guest arrived to start the party.

If not, he'd just have to make certain to give him an even better show to make up for starting without him. He was certain he could think of something. The thought of having her mouth around him as he slammed into the back of her throat almost forced a groan from him as his dick got harder.

His pleasure was almost ruined as he decided she would probably use her teeth in an attempt to hurt him. A smile crept onto his lips as he decided he'd just have to use his fist if she bit him. A few black eyes, or bruises on her cheek should quickly remind her that he wouldn't be trifled with, and have her working eagerly to please him.

CR80

Duncan looked over at Jake. "Drive faster."

"I'm already over the speed limit." One glance at Duncan and he mumbled, "Fine." Beneath him, the truck increased in speed. "But you're paying for my ticket, and bailing me out of jail."

"Done."

Duncan wanted to sag with relief that Melissa wasn't hurt, but he wasn't sure how long she'd remain that way. Even if the man didn't touch her, there was so much he could do that could cause irreparable damage.

It had only taken visits to two of the local thug hang outs before word began spreading like wildfire through the streets. Duncan would have laughed when the second gang leader pissed himself as he held him against the wall, flashing his fangs, but the situation was too serious. He was too afraid for Mel. Twenty minutes later they had found someone who knew where Travis was.

The asshole had thought he'd be able to use the information to extort money from him. Duncan sent Jake for his piercing bag. Using one of the needles, Duncan managed to convince the man he was not to be trifled with after his ear was pinned to the concrete sidewalk. When he showed the man the second needle, he started telling Duncan and Jake everything they wanted to know.

Duncan shook his head. He remembered when guys who called themselves "men" had a much higher pain threshold. But for now he couldn't help being grateful that the man gave in so easily.

Jake pulled up in front of the warehouse their informant said Travis was staying at.

"You stay here. I don't want you involved in this. When Melissa comes out, you take her to the club, make sure she gets to her brother." Pulling Jake's piercing kit on his lap, Duncan pulled out a few more needles.

"What about you?"

"Don't worry about me. Cause I'm not coming out until this bastard has paid."

C380

"Nice try. You were a much better actress when you were younger. I know you're awake."

Melissa tried not to shiver. She tried not to show any sign she was awake.

A slap threw her head to the side and she instantly tried to curl into a ball, her eyes flying open when she couldn't move.

"I knew you were awake."

"What's going on?" She strained against her bonds, her muscles trembling as she tried to pull them closer.

"Pay back. Now, all I need for this to be perfect is that freak of nature you call a brother to come rescue you. I'm ready for him this time." Travis displayed a large silver cross hidden beneath his shirt.

She wanted to laugh. She wanted to tell him that would have about as much of an effect on Gareth as baby powder would, but she kept her mouth shut.

"So, you've become quite the high class slut haven't you? Look at you all dressed up. Where were you going? Whoring yourself out for his friends? What are you, some kind of pampered pet?"

"Whatever I am, I'm still too good for you," she told him, unable to take his taunts in silence any longer.

"Bitch." He slapped her again. "Show some respect for your father."

"You're not my father," she screamed.

"Just like your mother."

"Thank you," she spit out.

When Travis noticed she wouldn't cower as she used to, he changed his tactics. "How very thoughtful of you. This will make it so much easier for me to have my fun. You don't think your pimp will mind if we start the party without him do you? I have been waiting twelve years for this."

"Don't you touch me!" She struggled against the ropes that kept her body spread out in the middle of the bed. She twisted and pulled until she could feel them biting into her flesh, could almost smell the blood from the fresh wounds.

"And who's going to stop me?" he asked with a smirk as his hand began to push her skirt higher.

"That would be me."

Travis froze at the voice behind him. Melissa followed his glance and saw Duncan leaning against a wall as though he didn't have a care in the world. She reached for him in her mind, seeking the warmth and comfort his presence always brought to her.

Instead, she felt as though she'd walked into a blizzard.

Chapter Fifteen

Duncan looked at the man who dared put his hands on Melissa. "You really don't want to make me ask you to take your hands off of her again."

"I don't remember you asking a first time. Who the hell do you think you are? This is none of your business," Travis said coldly, inching to the side.

"I'm the last person you're going to see in this life. But don't worry, you'll be happy to descend to the pits of hell when I'm through."

"Like I haven't heard that before. So what, are you, her new master?" Turning his head, Travis asked Melissa, "So is this the man you're whoring yourself to these days?"

Duncan slowly approached the bed Melissa was tied to, his face carefully arranged so he wouldn't look like he posed a threat. "It's not nice for you to talk to her like that. And you really don't want to touch her again."

"Who's going to stop me? You?" Travis laughed. "Answer me, you whore." He struck her again.

A quick glance at Melissa told Duncan her eyes were closed. He knew she would be humiliated because he saw her stepfather acting like that. He wanted to comfort her, but that would have to come later. First, he needed to teach this bastard some manners.

When Travis laid his hand on her thigh again, Duncan struck. Moving lightning fast, he moved behind Travis and jerked the man's hand off her. Yanking the man away from her, he pushed him down and knelt on his forearm. A smile curved his lips as he separated one finger from the group.

Positioning his fingers just so, he felt the bone snap and Travis screamed in pain.

"See, I told you not to touch her again. You look like a hard learner to me. You like to learn things the hard way, don't you? Allow me to give you a quick lesson." He gripped another finger. "You do not ever talk to a lady like that, but more importantly, you never, ever put your hands on her." Snap. "It's wrong."

Duncan released the broken finger. "Now, tell her you're sorry."

"Fuck you and that little bitch."

"Wrong answer." Snap. He broke a third finger. "Let's try again, but I will warn you. I have all the time in the world, but you only have so many bones. And if I get through them all, well, I'm gonna have to start all over again.

"You would be surprised at just how much pain the human body can feel. Just how much can be inflicted before you pass out. And there's so much more stuff we have to discuss, I'd hate to see you reduced to crying like a baby over a simple apology. Now…" he lifted the man's pinky, "…apologize for calling her a whore."

"I'm sorry, I'm sorry," Travis screamed as Duncan began to apply pressure to the finger.

"Good. I can see we're getting somewhere. Now, I'm going to untie the lady, and she's going to walk out of here while we continue our lessons. A smart man would stay right here."

Duncan rose to his feet and began to untie the rope around her ankle.

Glancing behind him discreetly, he saw Travis reach for a lead pipe, gripping it in his right hand as he held his broken fingers on his left hand close to his body.

Reaching inside his pocket, Duncan pulled out the cell phone he'd "borrowed" from the thug who told him where to find Travis and dialed Jake's number.

Sidestepping, he turned, curling his left hand into a fist and pushing it up into the man's stomach. The pipe fell from his hand and hit the ground with a clang. "You really aren't the sharpest tool in the shed are you?" He chuckled. "I've wanted to say that for years. The last time I had this kind of fun, no one used that phrase." He pushed him into a table, enjoying the way the man's eyes went wide as he was slowly stalked.

Behind him a door opened. Without turning around, Duncan spoke. "Jake, untie Melissa and make sure she gets home safe."

"Duncan." Her voice was pleading. "Come with us."

"No, Angel. He needs to be taught some manners."

"I won't leave without you," she told him stubbornly.

"Love, you don't have a choice. There are a few things I'd like to say to Travis here, that you really don't need to see."

"Don't—don't you mean hear?" Travis stuttered.

"No. I talk with my hands." He smirked. "I'm much more articulate that way."

"I'm not leaving." There was a small scuffle behind him and he heard Jake groan.

He had to fight back a chuckle. Returning his concentration to the man still trying to slither away, Duncan decided to outline his plan. With any luck, Melissa would faint or leave without seeing him put it into action.

Reaching into his pocket, he pulled out one of the needles he'd taken from Jake's bag.

"Is that supposed to scare me?" Travis laughed.

"Oh, it will. Using only this, I plan to peel the skin from your body. Don't worry, I won't work in one area too long. You see," he said, tilting the needle, "the trick is, if you use something too sharp, the body goes into shock much too fast. It has to be just dull enough to keep you feeling pain, but not enough to let you become unconscious.

"After I finish that, well, then the real fun will begin. But first, I plan on breaking half the bones in your body."

"Only half?" Travis sneered.

"Of course. The fun of torture depends on your victim being awake to feel it."

The color drained from Travis's face.

"What the fuck did I ever do to you?"

"I suppose you deserve to know. You see that beautiful woman, standing beside my friend? You hurt her." Moving lightning fast again, he grabbed Travis's shirt. "You dared to put your hands on her." Duncan punched him in the stomach. "You stole her childhood." His fist connected with the man's nose and the bone shattered. "You tried to steal her innocence. You tried to steal everything from her, and I will see that you pay for that with blood." He knocked the man to the floor and stomped on his leg with so much force he heard a pop. "Unfortunately, I'm not sure you have enough blood in your body. So we'll have to find a way to make up the difference."

"Duncan, stop," Melissa pleaded. He felt her behind him as he picked Travis up from the ground. "He isn't worth it."

"As long as he's alive he's going to try to hurt you. Go to the truck with Jake, Angel. I promise I'll be out there in a couple of minutes. You shouldn't have to see this."

"This isn't who you are." Her hand rested on his biceps. "Don't."

"This is exactly who I am. This is the real me, Angel. Nobody fucks with the people I love and walks away."

"You love me?"

Darting his eyes to her, he responded, his voice filled with the depth of his feelings for her. "More than I've ever loved anyone in my life."

"Then don't become a monster. He isn't worth it. Leave here with me. Take me back to your room and make me forget he ever existed."

Looking at her had been a mistake. He couldn't deny her anything, especially when she looked at him that way. As much as he wanted to snap the little man bleeding on him in half, he couldn't refuse anything Melissa asked of him. Pushing Travis back with as much force as he could, he growled, "You owe her your life."

"Take me home, Duncan. Take me home and help me forget."

He pulled her into his arms and nodded against her hair. "Only for you Angel. I'll let him live for *you*."

Turning Duncan put his arm around her and walked toward Jake.

"Duncan," Jake called, but it was a second too late. Beside him, Melissa stiffened, her eyes wide with shock, filled with pain. Jake rushed toward them. Looking down, Duncan saw a butterfly knife sticking out of her back. Duncan cradled her to his body.

"I love you, Duncan," she whispered, before she lost consciousness in his arms.

"It doesn't look like anything major was hit," Jake said. "If we can close the wound, she should survive."

Jake held her as Duncan pulled the knife from her body, quickly placing his tongue over the wound. Closing his eyes, Duncan prayed to all of the gods he'd ever heard of that she survived. After several swipes, he was about to give up hope when the wound began to slowly close. He continued to concentrate on healing her.

He didn't stop until it was completely closed. The only proof she'd ever been injured was in the blood still on her flesh. Much to his relief, he watched her chest rise and fall, though the action was much slower than he'd like.

"Get her to her brother, he'll be at Club Strigoi."

"Shouldn't I take her to a hospital?"

Duncan shook his head. "Take her to Gareth. He'll know if she needs to go to the hospital. Tell him her bastard of a stepfather will never bother her again." Jake gathered Melissa closer to him. "This wipes the slate for us," Duncan told him seriously. "If anything, I'm in debt to you."

"Duncan..."

"Get her to safety. Get her to her brother."

Without saying a word, Jake gently picked up Melissa. Before he stepped away, Duncan placed a tender kiss on her lips. "I love you, Angel."

He waited until Jake left the room. If anyone asked, he would be able to respond with complete honesty that Travis was still alive when he last saw him.

All games were over. Duncan picked up the butterfly knife he'd removed from Melissa's back and stalked his prey.

"She saved your life. She spared you and you repay her kindness by trying to kill her." Duncan gave one quick jab, smiling when Travis looked down at the blade sticking out of the center of his chest. "I hope you rot in hell."

"I'll take comfort in the fact that you'll be joining me." Travis coughed, blood leaking from his mouth.

"Maybe. The gods know I deserve to go there. But every time I see your face, I'll know that at least I protected an angel from you." Deciding that the other man wasn't dying quickly enough, Duncan grasped the knife and twisted it sharply. He watched with pride as the other man's lifeless body fell to the floor.

ᙅ൩ᙣ

He didn't bother to change his clothes. He walked straight to Gareth's house from the warehouse. There wasn't much time before dawn, but he had to know if she was all right. He had to know if she would survive, or if he'd be beating the shit out of her stepfather in hell that day.

Lalita opened the door and ushered him inside the house before running to get Gareth.

When he appeared, he held his hand out to Duncan. When he reached for it, Gareth pulled him into a hug.

"You saved her life." His voice was thick with emotion. "She'll be weak for a few days, but she'll survive. If you hadn't been there…"

Duncan shook his head. He refused to think about what would have happened if he hadn't shown up. If he did, he'd only beat the shit out of himself for letting that bastard stepfather of hers die so quickly.

Sandy Lynn

Now that he had his answer about Melissa's condition, he turned toward the door.

"What are you doing?"

"You were right. I don't deserve her. I never deserved her. But I will thank the gods every day that she allowed me to be a part of her life, even if only for a short time." Reaching into his pocket he handed Gareth the velvet box.

"Thanks but I'm already spoken for. And you're not really my type."

"Give this to Mel for me."

"Give it to her yourself." He pressed the box back into Duncan's hand.

Duncan shook his head and placed it on the counter. "I'm a monster. Tonight proves that beyond any shadow of doubt. I'm a villain, and we all know the villains don't get the girl in the end." Turning, he walked out of the house.

Chapter Sixteen

"Duncan," Melissa called as she woke up.

"He's not here," Gareth answered.

"Why? He told me he'd stay with me. You two didn't fight did you?" Melissa propped herself up on the bed. "What happened?" she asked when she saw the bags under his eyes.

"You almost died, Mel."

"No. Duncan saved me. Travis only slapped me a few times. You'd have been proud of him. I think he really would have killed that bastard. He loves me Gareth. Please don't be mad I didn't call you. You haven't had any of my blood in the last few weeks so you wouldn't have heard me."

"I know, baby, I know." He pulled her into a hug.

"Why aren't you mad? What aren't you telling me?" She pushed against him, forcing him away from her so she could see his face. "Tell me what happened," she demanded.

"Travis stabbed you. He threw a knife and it hit you. Duncan saved your life. If he hadn't closed your wound…"

"Where is he?" She looked around her bedroom as though expecting him to pop up and yell surprise.

"He wanted me to give you this. He's gone Mel." Gareth handed her a small black velvet box.

"Is he… Is he…" Tears rolled down her cheeks and she couldn't finish the question.

"No, baby, he's fine. He said he didn't deserve you."

"I'm gonna kick his ass." She began to struggle to get out of bed.

"Easy, take it easy, sis."

"He thinks he can save me one night then the next night he can just walk away without even letting me know he wasn't hurt. Why the hell can't I get out of bed?"

"You're still weak. You've been asleep for almost two days."

"Then help me out of this bed. I've got an ass to go kick."

"It's good to see that she's feeling better," Lalita chuckled.

"Gareth, get out. La can help me. Then we are going to the club and that man is going to be sorry he got out of bed tonight."

She tossed the box on the nightstand beside her lamp.

"Aren't you even going to open it?"

"Nope. He can give it to me, or he can shove it up his ass."

"Yup, she's feeling better." Gareth gave her a hug, holding her so tight she thought he was going to break her ribs.

"Give him hell, Mel."

Once Gareth was out of the room, she attempted to climb out of the bed again.

"So, what do you want to wear?"

"I don't care, anything. I just want to give that bastard a piece of my mind."

CR80

Duncan was watching the screens. He kept glancing at a couple near the center of the dance floor who looked like they were either in the middle of a fight or about to fuck on the floor. Concentrating on them, he hadn't been able to figure out which mode they were in, yet.

Behind him the door opened.

"For the last time, I don't need to be relieved. I'm quite happy with control room duty, so leave me the fuck alone." He winced as something hit the back of his head, hard. "What the fu—"

Turning, he saw the small box on the floor. Looking up slowly he devoured the sight of Melissa standing in the doorway with her hands on her hips, only slightly stunned that she'd gotten past him on the monitors. Then again, considering the way that one couple had been acting, maybe it wasn't such a surprise.

"Shove that up your ass."

"I thought you'd like it. I thought it'd look perfect on you."

"Fuck you. You want to give me something then you give it to me. Don't ask my brother to do it for you."

"Mel, I—you deserve to be with someone that's much better than I'll ever be."

"Fuck you. Don't boss me around. I'm so glad to know I meant so goddamn much to you." From the fury in her eyes, he was glad she didn't have anything else to throw at him. "You've had your fun, the least you could do is be a man and break up with me in person. I want to hear you say it. I want to hear you say you were just playing me, just like my brother knew you were."

"I wasn't playing with you."

"No, you had to be playing with me. Because if you weren't...if you weren't..."

At that moment nothing could have stopped him from holding her in his arms. Approaching her, his arms open, he was surprised when she slapped him instead of stepping into his embrace.

"What was that for?" he growled.

"You are an asshole."

He stepped closer, wrapping his arms around her.

"Don't touch me. Don't you ever touch me again! You're a liar. You're nothing but a filthy liar and I'm through with you. Get away from me." She struggled weakly in his arms, kicking and twisting, fighting his embrace.

"Gods, Angel," he whispered in her ear before her foot came down on top of his. He had missed her so much.

Tears shined in her eyes as she slapped him across the face again. "Don't call me that. You lied to me. You lied."

Guilt flooded him. He had promised her that he wouldn't let Travis touch her, but the bastard had managed to not only slap her, but to stab her. He couldn't blame her for being mad.

"You swore you'd always be there for me. You swore you wouldn't leave me." She slapped him a third time. "You promised I wouldn't be alone and then you left me."

"Angel, I'm so sorry." He let her beat her fists against his chest. "If I'd known—if I'd even thought that bastard would be waiting for you, I would have been right there beside you."

"No, not then. I woke up and you were gone. I tried to find you, but you were gone. You blocked me from your mind, and had my brother give me something you bought for me. You used me. You lied to me."

Her legs began to shake beneath her and he scooped her up, enjoying how she felt so close to him.

Sitting down with her on his lap, he tried to explain. "I don't deserve you."

"What about me? What do I deserve? Do I deserve to have what I want?"

"You deserve a man that will make you happy, not one that scares you. I saw the fear in your eyes in that warehouse. You deserve a man that can be everything that you want."

"But all I want is you."

"Angel..."

She interrupted him. "Do you love me? Just answer that. Do you love me, Duncan?"

Looking into her eyes, he knew she would leave if he said no. If he told her no, she'd walk away and find a man that deserved her. But he couldn't lie to her.

"I love you more than I've ever loved anything."

"Then don't deny me the one thing I want. Don't tell me I can't be with the only man I've ever loved. Well, the only man other than my brother."

She pulled him down to her mouth. "Make me warm again. I want to feel warm and safe again."

Her tongue slid over his lips, then into his mouth. He wanted to be strong and push her away so she could find a better man, but the thought made him groan. He could feel her trying to find him through the ice he had placed between them. He could feel her reaching out for him.

Unable to stand the distance between them, he destroyed the wall, sighing into her mouth as he felt her surrounding him.

"I can't do this," he told her when their kiss ended.

She looked at him and nodded. Standing up, she stepped away from him.

Reaching on the floor behind the chair, he picked up the box she'd thrown at him. Before she could walk through the door, he called her.

"Melissa?"

"What?" She paused but didn't turn around.

"Will you look at me please?"

"What?" Her voice filled with anger and pain.

He waited until she was watching him before he approached her. Kneeling in front of her, he opened the small box and lifted it to her.

"Will you marry me? Will you become a vampire and spend the rest of our lives kicking my ass when I act like an idiot?"

"Duncan..."

"I tried to be strong. I tried to let you go so you could find a better man, but all I really want is to spend the rest of my life with you. You have done what no one else in history has ever been able to do. You are the only person to ever bring me to my knees."

She sniffed, a single tear rolling down her cheek. "Not the most romantic proposal in the world."

"I told you I suck at this shit. But I promise to stay beside you, to love you, and to seriously fuck up anyone who tries to hurt you."

She laughed and jumped into his arms, sending them both flying backward. He kissed her greedily, chuckling as he felt her hands tugging on his shirt.

"Does this mean you accept?"

"Yes, I do."

Duncan pulled the ring from the box and slid it onto her finger. "I knew it would be perfect." He kissed the back of her hand and tried to pull her down to him.

"I believe you owe me something else."

"I won't apologize for what happened with Travis," he told her firmly.

"No. I believe you taunted me with the fact that you were getting a certain piercing. Now, I want to see it."

He chuckled as she climbed off him.

"I want to see it," she told him again, sitting down in the chair, waiting for him to move. He removed his jeans, and stood in front of her with his cock in front of her face.

She ran her finger over the barbells, before rubbing them against her cheek. Her mouth closed over him and she giggled as she slowly pulled back. "That's going to take a little getting used to. Guess this means I'm going to have to get plenty of practice."

He groaned. "Angel, you are killing me."

"Not yet. Thank you for saving me Duncan." She stood up and quickly shed her clothes. "Now, come here so I can thank you properly."

He groaned when she pushed him down into the chair. Watching her glide across the room, he smiled when she locked the door then returned to him.

Climbing onto the chair, she lowered herself onto him. "That feels…nice…" she moaned.

Kissing her neck, he cupped her ass as she lifted herself until only the tip of his cock was still buried within her then slowly lowered herself again. "It's definitely nice," she told him huskily.

"Angel…" He wanted so badly to be buried completely inside her, to taste her blood but was afraid it was too soon for that.

"Only if I can taste you, too," she told him as her pace increased slightly. "I want to be a vampire."

Nodding, Duncan lifted his wrist to his mouth and pierced through the flesh then presented it to her. He groaned as she drank slowly from him, her tongue swirling over the opening. Her pace increased as she pulled away from him, a little trail dripping down her chin. He closed the wound and kissed her hungrily.

His mouth trailed over her cheek to her neck. After one hard pull with his mouth, his teeth sank into her. Her pussy began to clench around him as his mouth filled with her blood. Duncan thrust hard up into her, trying to resist the urge to come. Seeing her head thrown back, hearing her moans ripped his control from him.

Still buried inside of her, Duncan kissed her gently.

"I love you Melissa. I will always love you."

"I love you too, my freaky baby."

Melissa looked behind her at the screens. "Looks like there's another couple in the back room."

He looked past her and chuckled. "Yeah, it does." It was the couple from the floor. Apparently, they had decided after all.

"Think you can keep up with them?"

"For you, I could do anything."

About the Author

To learn more about Sandy Lynn, please visit www.SandyLynn.com. Send an email to Sandy at sandy@sandylynn.com or join her Yahoo. group to join in the fun with other readers as well as Sandy.

http://groups.yahoo.com/group/Club_Strigoi/

He's gorgeous, he's got great manners, he's got a mission to accomplish. The only drawback? He's been dead for a hundred years.

Not Quite Dead
© 2006 Sela Carsen

Sabine Harper's night started out badly—a dead man jumped out of his grave, she was chased by a vampire and now she has an uninvited guest. The worst part? A guy who may or may not be entirely dead is looking ten times better than any living man she's ever dated.

Willem Breaux has only three days to avenge his murder, but upon awakening more than a century into the future, he discovers that he needs Sabine's help more than he could have imagined. And in the end, he'll need her love more than anything else.

Can Willem and Sabine find love—and a little laughter—in spite of time, death and an evil that's waited a century to make its move?

Available now in ebook and print from Samhain Publishing.

Enjoy the following excerpt from Not Quite Dead...

"What's your name?"

"Sabine Harper."

"Sabine." One muscled arm reached past her and picked up the lamp. He shone it directly into her face. "Your hair is too dark. And your eyes should be brown."

"Well, they're not. That's what I've been trying to tell you." Fear evaporated to be replaced with fury.

He was silent. The anger in his own face melted away, leaving a stoic mask.

"The blonde who was with you. Who is she?"

"That's Lily. She's my cousin." Sensation rushed back to limbs gone numb with terror. Nerves pricked painfully in her head and blood pounded at her temple. "She and her stupid little friends were playing a game tonight, mumbling spells, trying to raise you from the dead. I can't believe it worked."

Willem shook his head. "It didn't work. Not unless she's Rose."

"I don't understand."

"Neither do I." He looked down at his hand on her arm and grimaced. "You might be Rose and you might not. How long have I been..."

"Dead?" she supplied. "How long have you been dead? According to your tombstone, over one hundred twenty years." Sarcasm dripped in her tone. This was ridiculous. Sabine wrenched away from his loosened grip. "If you knew a Rose during your lifetime, I can pretty much guarantee she's dead, too. Unless she's decided to go for a little walk tonight and stretch out her decayed skeleton. Who are you anyway?"

"My name is Willem Breaux. This used to be my house."

She muttered an oath. "Great. Just great. Vampires, the walking dead, and now I live in a haunted house."

"It's haunted?" He leaned back from her.

"You're here, aren't you?" Sabine took deep breaths, keeping her eyes on the man who had invaded her home. His home. Whatever.

"Why, exactly, are you here?" she asked.

Willem rose stiffly and wandered over to the French doors leading to her spacious back yard. "I'm here to kill St. Ivraie."

"Who?"

"Richard St. Ivraie. The vampire you saw tonight."

"Fan-freakin'-tastic. Vampires. Dead man walking. I have completely lost my mind. You are a figment of my twisted imagination, right? That's it. No more Stephen King movies on late night cable."

"I beg your pardon?"

Sabine sighed and tried again. "You know what? Just for fun, I'm going to go along with this. I'm going to pretend this is real to see if my subconscious is trying to tell me something important." She took a deep breath and pasted a patient smile on her face. "Okay. You've been dead for over a hundred years. Why now? Why after all this time?"

"Because he's back. He stole my woman, turned her, and she murdered me. This time it's my turn."

Sabine snorted indelicately. "Nice. I thought vengeance was the Lord's." She rose and he followed her into the kitchen.

"I'm not a ghost," he said, as if that would help.

Sabine filled her tea kettle with water. It soothed to her to go through the simple ritual during troubling times. "What are you?"

"I'm not sure." He leaned against her counter and watched her assemble cups and teabags while she waited for the water to heat.

There was nothing left for her to do with her hands and she stopped. She turned to focus on him. There was a ghoul—imaginary, but very male—standing in her kitchen. He was dirty, but otherwise didn't look as though he had lain decomposing for over a century. Maybe he wasn't a ghoul.

He was something, though. His hair was probably dark blond under the dirt and since his clothing hung in rags, she had a pretty good idea that he had lived an active life, if his muscles were anything to go by.

The shrill whistle of the kettle broke the silence. Sabine poured hot water over her teabag, then hesitated. "I don't know if you drink, or eat, or sleep. Should I pour you a cup of tea?"

"Yes, please."

A ghoul with manners.

He smiled at her and he was beautiful. Fully male with a charming twinkle in his eyes. She shuddered and turned away as tears sprang again to her eyes.

"Are you all right?" he asked. Since they'd come into the kitchen he had watched her closely, examining her body, her hair, her face.

"Sure. I'm not usually a crier, but it's been kind of a rough night. Anyway, it's okay to cry during psychotic breaks." She turned a half smile on him over her shoulder. Then, as if she entertained cadavers all the time, took the teabags out of the cups and asked if he wanted milk or honey.

He barely waited for the burning liquid to cool before he began drinking. The taste of something must have awakened his appetite because his stomach rumbled like the vibrating of a bass fiddle. She looked over at him. He might have flushed, but she couldn't tell under the dust.

"Hungry?" she asked, smiling into her mug.

His lips tilted up and he put his empty cup on the counter. "Now that you mention it, I could do with something to eat."

"As long as you don't want to drink my blood or snack on my soul, I think I can fix you up."

He ran his thumb under his lip as if to check for fangs. The dark gleam in his eyes, combined with the sensually assessing look on his face, made Sabine's body tingle in a rush from head to toe. Not a ghoul. Definitely male. And so Sabine found herself frying eggs and ham at four o'clock in the morning for a man who had died generations before she was born.

Will this Elven warlord be conquered by lust?

Lords of Ch'i
© 2006 Ciar Cullen

Cast out by an usurper to her clan's throne, warrior Silver SanMartin throws herself at the mercy of her compelling enemy, Jet Atraud. The sexy warlord rules his Elven clan with an iron fist, but Silver finds she lords some power of her own. Jet can't keep his eyes—or his hands—off his lovely captive.

In a battle to gain self-control and maintain his ten-year oath of celibacy, Jet tries to focus on the task at hand—conquering the enemy clans. Despite his strong will and best intentions, Jet cannot ignore his growing love for Silver. But can a sworn enemy be trusted?

Available now in ebook and print from Samhain Publishing.

Enjoy the following excerpt from Lords of Ch'i…

Silver looked up again, and a shock of electricity ran through her at Jet's intense stare. He looked from her eyes to her lips, and let his gaze wander to her breasts, pushed high by her gown. His eyes burned as she he assaulted her senses.

"You're rather strong-willed, Silver. I don't buy your apology for a second. And I think I rather fancy that about you. You'll make a good bodyguard. What do you think of the gown? It's been in my family for many generations."

"Lord?"

"Yes?" He continued his sexual appraisal of her and her breathing quickened in longing. She let her gaze wander down his smooth stomach to his rigid cock, straining against the black silk wrap. *Surely he can hear my heart, it's so loud.*

"Do you like what you see, Silver? You can't seem to pull your gaze away for long. Do you know the whole time we've spoken, the whole time you've cried over the conflict and your brother, you've filled the room with your lust. You've stared at my mouth and my chest, my stomach, wondering how it would feel, how it would be between us. Am I wrong?"

"You are quite wrong, Lord."

He laughed a little and motioned her to come closer. "I'd like a closer look at you in my ancestor's garb. You must admit, it suits your figure, which is…" Jetre took in a quick breath. "Adequate."

"Adequate? My figure is adequate? Why are we discussing my body? Your oath, your…"

"Have I broken my oath, Silver?" He worked his fingertips from her collarbone across the swell of her breasts. His touch blazed a fiery trail across her skin and his energy seeped into her veins. *Which burns,* she wondered—*the touch of an elf or the touch of a lord?* He slowly unfastened the clasps of her dress until he exposed her breasts. His calloused fingers and palms brushed across her skin like a kiss as he cupped one breast in each hand. His moan stirred her to quivering. He caressed her as if he'd found a priceless treasure he'd sought for a lifetime. Silver fought the sensations he evoked, but surrendered and cried out when he rubbed his thumbs on her nipples.

"Jetre."

"Yes?" He continued his slow circles. "You find this unpleasant? Should I stop?" Jetre looked at her from beneath his dark lashes as he leaned in to suckle on one breast. His hot mouth assaulted her senses, his tongue darting across her nipple, his lips pulling and pinching. A low groaning sound came from far away, and Silver realized in shock it was her moan, her lust filling the air. She laced her hands in an errant strand of his luxurious hair and pulled it towards her face, smelling his scent—dark spices and male magic. When he moved to her other breast, the new pleasure sent her to the brink of orgasm, and he kept her hovered there for minutes. He broke away suddenly and looked into her eyes.

Silver panted, aching, throbbing, ready to push him to the ground and assault him. "You're no virgin."

"How dare you. Do you understand how you insult me, Warrior?"

"I honestly couldn't tell you what I think right now if my life depended upon it."

Jetre arched a brow. "It will come to you."

Silver's hands shook at the conflicting, overwhelming emotions consuming her. This man, this gorgeous man, her sworn enemy, now her master—was he seducing her? No, simply playing with his prisoner. No more, certainly. A tiny dagger of regret pierced her heart. Silver shuddered, the memory of his mouth on her still making her tingle, still making her throb and moist and ready.

What I wouldn't give to lay with him, to feel him inside me... She cursed to herself. Too late, he heard it.

"Tell me, let me hear what you want." His voice grew low and languid, his eyes nearly hidden beneath his black lashes. "Tell me what kind of lover you imagine me? What draws you? My look? My manner? Or my power?"

All of those. None of those. Don't let him hear any more. Thoughts poured out, desire and longing overwhelming her, betraying her.

You're the most beautiful creature. Take me now or leave me be. I don't want to feel this way.

"Yes you do." His voice was such a low whisper Silver thought she might have imagined hearing him speak.

Jet sat up straight, eyes now wide, spell broken. "I'm not one to take advantage of my position with a woman, with anyone. You aren't required to placate me in a sexual way." Jetre snorted. "Perhaps that's only my ego. I couldn't stand the thought of forcing myself on a woman. I've always assumed no woman would reject me, which is quite disturbing. Perhaps you don't want me?"

Silver groaned. "Don't mock me, Lord, you read my thoughts clearly enough. It's bad enough that I've betrayed my kind. Don't make me betray myself."

Jetre ignored her words and stood, pulling the cord from his hair.

That's his way? Play with me for a moment, send my world reeling, and dismiss me like a scrap of garbage.

"You'll help me dress now, and we will eat and drink with the soldiers and their families. I intend to speak to the crowd of your presence here. Some of it will annoy you, badly, especially when I speak of your brother. Try to show restraint. Understood?"

"Yes, Lord."

He turned and nodded. "Silver, in private, you may call me Jet. I'm a little less formal than most of the lords." He held out a finger. "In private, mind you."

She nodded. "Jet." She tested the nickname on her tongue.

"One thing." Jetre turned away again. His voice was quiet and Silver struggled to hear him. "Was it right? Did it feel right, what I did? When I kissed your breasts?"

It was the last question she expected from him, the most amazing thing. The great Lord Jetre, wondering if he had given her any pleasure. *How to answer him?*

"Because my ten years end in a matter of days." He pushed his hand through his hair and laughed at himself. "I don't want it said the oath made the lord incapable. How embarrassing. Is this your nature—to bring out the inner truths of a person?"

"How will I protect you from the women who will storm your quarters when your oath is complete? They'll be more dangerous than Fire and Metal combined against you." *And how will I bear to watch it?*

Jet laughed. "As appealing as that picture might be, I must pick only one. The second part of the deal." He shrugged.

"I see." A small knife poked at her heart unexpectedly. No doubt the woman would be Wood and was probably already betrothed to the lord. An elf, of course.

"You didn't answer my question." Jet toweled down and Silver turned away. From the corner of her eye she saw him step into his dark leather pants and pull on a thin, collarless, long-sleeved, black shirt. He went to the dresser and placed a kohl stick against each eye, blinking and wiping the excess from his cheeks.

"The woman will be quite fortunate, Jet. I hope that satisfies your ego."

He inclined his head and smiled very subtly. "It does. Might I practice on you again some time?"

Silver closed her eyes. The pain came in very faintly, like the smell of a coming summer rain shower on the breeze. She wanted her sworn enemy, and she meant nothing to him. A plaything, a practice toy. *Well, there are worse fates than being the whore of such a man.*

He pointed to his tall boots and Silver brought them to him, helped him push into them.

"You did something terrible to me when you branded me, Jet. I know you did. You say you wouldn't force a woman, but you charmed me in some way."

Jet looked up at her, puzzled. "Nonsense."

"I don't believe you."

Jet pointed to the dresser and his heavy, white-gold pendant, the Wu Xing symbol of his clan, the symbol of the Way of Ch'i. Silver brought it to him and fastened it around his neck. She bit back thoughts of Kilé and how she had fastened his pendant many times.

"Not many call me a liar without punishment. If Jaine or Art were here, you'd already be bleeding."

"Yes, my lord. Based on my brief encounter with your formidable sister, I believe you."

"Now my hair."

"What about it?"

"Brush it." He rolled his eyes at her.

"This is fucking awful, Lord."

"You'll get used to it."

Silver went to the dresser, grabbed a brush, and pulled a cushion behind Jetre's. She brushed his beautiful hair, wishing she could bury her face in it.

He turned suddenly and grabbed her by the neck. "I heard that."

She cried out softly, even though he didn't hurt her.

"They'll have to wait a few minutes more."

Samhain Publishing, Ltd.

It's all about the story…

Interested in writing for us?

Samhain Publishing is open to all submissions and seeks well-written works that engage the reader. We encourage the author to let their muse have its way and to create tales that don't always adhere to trends. One never knows what the next trend will be or when it will start, so write what's in your soul. These are the books that, whether the story is based on "formula" or an "original", are written from the heart, and can keep you up reading all night!

For details, go to http:

www.samhainpublishing.com/submissions.shtml

Samhain Publishing, Ltd.

It's all about the story...

Action/Adventure

Fantasy

Historical

Horror

Mainstream

Mystery/Suspense

Non-Fiction

Paranormal

Red Hots!

Romance

Science Fiction

Western

Young Adult

http://www.samhainpublishing.com